D0934574

Of Paupers and Peers

Of Paupers and Peers

Sheri Cobb South

Five Star • Waterville, Maine

First Edition
First Printing: September 2006

Published in 2006 in conjunction with Tekno Books.

Set in 11 pt. Plantin by Myrna S. Raven.

Printed in the United States on permanent paper.

Library of Congress Cataloging-in-Publication Data

South, Shari Cobb.
    Of paupers and peers / by Shari Cobb South—1st ed.
    p. cm.
    ISBN 1-59414-529-6 (hc : alk. paper)
    1. Clergy—Fiction.   2. Inheritance and succession—
Fiction.   3. Amnesia—Fiction.   4. Mistaken identity—
Fiction.   I. Title.
PS3569.O755O35 2006
    813´.54—dc22
                                                        2006015848

To Elizabeth White, critique partner extraordinaire.

PROLOGUE

It was not with the intention of disobliging his family that Lord Robert Weatherly, in the year of our Lord seventeen hundred and twenty-five, fell in love with a dairymaid, although a moment's reasoning must have been sufficient to inform him that his Molly, whatever her charms, could hardly be thought a suitable match for a son—even a younger son—of the fourth duke of Montford. But in the end it was love, not reason, that carried the day, and so Lord Robert carried his blushing bride to the altar. His father, the duke, celebrated the nuptials with a visit to the office of his solicitor, where he derived a certain satisfaction in drawing up a new will in which his second son was cut off without a shilling.

The scandal of Lord Robert's *mésalliance* was eventually forgotten, as such scandals invariably are once more recent *on dits* drive them from public memory, but the duke never relented. An excruciatingly correct letter from Lord Robert to his father two years later notified the latter of the birth of his grandson, but this was never acknowledged, and communication between the two houses ceased. Eventually the elder branch of the family was able to forget the shame visited upon it by the simple expedient of ignoring the younger's existence. Lord Robert's descendants, for their part, had little time to waste in dwelling on such matters, occupied as they were with earning their bread.

And so the noble connection grew more tenuous with each generation that passed, to such an extent that fully a century later, when the ninth duke of Montford passed on to his eternal reward, the College of Arms was obliged to embark upon a four-month search to locate the tenth duke. But locate him they did at last, in the form of one Mr. James Weatherly, great-great-grandson of that long-ago fourth duke, and at present serving as curate of Fairford parish.

Informed of this discovery, Mr. Henry Mayhew, solicitor to the late duke, was dispatched at once from London to Fairford. Upon being set down at the local posting-house (for Fairford only offered one, being little more than a village), he obtained a room for the night and lingered there only long enough to remove the dust of travel from his person before setting out for Mr. Weatherly's residence. This humble dwelling proved to be a hired room over a chandler's shop.

"Is Mr. Weatherly in, please?" he inquired of the proprietress, a buxom woman with a maternal air.

"Aye, he is, but he's giving a lesson," was her unpromising response.

"May I at least arrange a time when I might see him?" Mr. Mayhew persisted. "I've come from London on a matter of some importance."

The proprietress crossed her arms over her substantial bosom and regarded her visitor with mingled suspicion and respect. "London, eh? Very well, follow me."

She led him through the back door of the shop and up a narrow staircase, which clung to the outside wall. As he neared the landing, Mr. Mayhew could hear the high-pitched voice of a young boy reciting declensions in labored Latin.

"Mensa, mensa, mensas—"

"Mensas?" a second voice gently questioned.

"Mensam," the young scholar hastily corrected himself. *"Mensae, mensae—"*

8

Without waiting for the end of the exercise, Mr. Mayhew's hostess rapped on the door.

"Come in," the more mature voice called from within.

"You've a visitor from London, Mr. Weatherly," that gentleman's landlady announced as she opened the door.

Both of the room's inhabitants looked up at the unexpected visitor. The pupil, a stout lad of seven, went so far as to bounce up from his chair at this welcome respite from his studies. It was not the boy, however, but his tutor who drew Mr. Mayhew's attention. A scholarly young man of twenty-seven, he was possessed of a countenance as gentle as his manner, with a rather long, thin face, fine blue eyes that might occasionally be seen to twinkle behind wire-rimmed spectacles, and golden locks that were prone to droop, as now, over his aristocratic brow. Indeed, he might have been accounted handsome, were it not for a rather prominent nose, which tended toward the concave. As he stood at his visitor's entrance, it became evident that he was exceptionally tall, and thin to the point of lankiness—a circumstance which accounted for the fact that the sleeves of his threadbare black coat did not quite reach his wrists.

Mr. Mayhew, noting this dreary garment, at first thought that Mr. Weatherly must already have received word of his noble cousin's demise. But a moment's reflection reminded him that sober attire was indicative, not of mourning, but of Mr. Weatherly's profession.

"Mr. James Weatherly?"

The younger man sketched a slight bow. "Yes. How may I serve you?"

Mr. Mayhew glanced uncertainly at the boy, and Mr. Weatherly, taking the hint, turned to address himself to his pupil. "You may go now, Thomas. Remember to study your declensions before next week's lesson."

The boy left the room readily enough, but Mr. Mayhew was obliged to give the proprietress, hovering expectantly just inside the doorway, a rather pointed look. She gave a little huff of indignation, then turned and clattered back down the stairs.

Alone with his visitor, Mr. Weatherly spoke to the solicitor. "Is something amiss, Mr.—?"

"Mayhew. And no, nothing is amiss."

The mild blue eyes twinkled. "You will never convince me that you made the journey from London merely for the pleasure of making my acquaintance!"

This drew a smile from the solicitor. "No, it is considerably more than that." He reached into his breast pocket and drew out a sheaf of papers. "It is my duty and privilege to inform you that you are now the duke of Montford."

CHAPTER 1

For a long moment James stared at the solicitor in stunned disbelief. Then, ever so gradually, the corners of his mouth turned up in a surprisingly sweet smile framed, incongruously, by a dimple in each lean cheek.

"Who put you up to this?" he asked knowingly. "One of my cronies from University, I'll be bound! Perry, perhaps, or Torrington. I haven't heard from either of them in years!"

"I assure you, your Grace, I was never more in earnest."

This lofty form of address had the effect of wiping the smile from James's face. "But this is impossible!"

"Not at all." Mr. Mayhew spread open his sheaf of papers, revealing a painstakingly transcribed family tree. "You are James Weatherly, only son of the late Arthur Weatherly, are you not?"

"Yes."

"Then there can be no doubt." The solicitor traced one finger along the genealogical chart. "Your father was the eldest son of Charles Robert Weatherly, who was the sole surviving son of Edward James Weatherly, who was the eldest son of Lord Robert Weatherly, second son of George Edward Arnold Weatherly, fourth duke of Montford."

This revelation caused James's jaw to drop, making his long, thin face even longer. Mr. Mayhew, seeing this reaction, was moved to inquire, "You truly did not know?"

The duke of Montford shook his head. "I had no idea. You are quite certain—yes, I see that you must be. I was orphaned at an early age, you see, and grew up among my mother's people. I know very little about my father's family."

"Your father may not have known himself precisely where he stood in the succession. I believe there was a falling out between the fourth duke and his younger son a century or more ago, which resulted in Lord Robert's being disinherited," Mr. Mayhew said. "Still, you must have encountered some of your Weatherly cousins while at school."

James shook his head dazedly. "No, never." He looked up sharply as a thought struck him. "If I've Weatherly cousins, wouldn't one of *them* be duke?"

"Indeed they would, if they were descendants of the fourth duke's eldest son. But the elder branch of the family produced no male heirs beyond the ninth duke, who died without issue last August. The cousins to whom I refer were descended from Lord Robert's younger brother. You are quite certain you never knew any of them at Oxford?"

"I was educated at Cambridge," James corrected him, "as was my father before me."

"Interesting," Mr. Mayhew acknowledged with a slight nod. "Oxford has been the university of choice for the Weatherlys for generations."

"If Lord Robert's quarrel with his father was as bitter as you suggest, that might explain why he chose to break with tradition," suggested James.

"Indeed, it might. But no matter how bitter the quarrel, the estate was entailed. No matter how he might have wished it, Montford could not prevent Lord Robert—or any of his issue—from inheriting both the title and the estate, should it ever fall to them."

"Estate?" echoed James, still struggling to take it in.

"Just over two million acres in Surrey," Mr. Mayhew informed him.

"Two—*million?*"

"Attached to the principal seat, yes. There are also smaller holdings in Somerset and Monmouth, but none of these is over a hundred thousand acres. You will no doubt wish to acquaint yourself with your holdings as soon as possible, so I have taken the liberty of withdrawing on your behalf the sum of fifty guineas, which I trust will allow you to travel in a manner befitting your station."

"Fifty guineas," echoed James numbly, accepting from Mr. Mayhew's hand a purse containing the equivalent of more than a year's wages.

Mr. Mayhew's eyebrows arched upwards in some concern. "If the sum is insufficient, I might—"

"No, no," James assured him hastily. "Fifty guineas will be—quite sufficient."

"I have also been charged to inform you that, should you choose to take your seat in the House of Lords, the earl of Torrington will be pleased to stand sponsor to you."

"The House of Lords!" echoed James in some alarm. "Good God! What will I do?"

Mr. Mayhew permitted himself a wry smile. "As to that, your Grace, you are a wealthy man and a peer of the realm. You may do precisely as you please."

The queer thing about being a duke, reflected James as he walked to the vicarage for his customary Wednesday dinner with the parish incumbent, was that one did not feel like a duke at all, but rather like a curate and occasional Latin tutor caught in a bizarre but vivid dream.

You may do precisely as you please . . . The phrase echoed in James's still-spinning head. *Precisely as you please . . .* But what *did* he please? He had never been at liberty to consider the question before; had he been asked, he would have supposed that someday he might be given the living at Fairford upon the current vicar's retirement, but with no money and no connections—no apparent connections, at any rate—he had never had reason to hope for more than this modest ambition.

"Ah, good evening, James," said the reverend Mr. John Bainbridge, opening the door to admit his assistant and frequent guest. "I trust I find you well?"

"Quite well, thank you," James assured him, shrugging his long arms out of his worn greatcoat. "The squire and his lady were good enough to send me a measure of coal for the fire, and there is hope that young Thomas may grasp Latin declensions yet. And a London solicitor called to inform me that I am the duke of Montford."

James had hoped that speaking the words aloud might imbue them with some sense of reality. It did not, but at least he had the felicity of gaining a partner in his disbelief. The reverend Mr. Bainbridge, removing a dented copper kettle from the fire, whirled 'round to confront his curate, pale eyes bulging in his wizened face.

"I—beg—your—pardon?"

"I am told there can be no mistake. You have the honor of addressing his Grace, the tenth duke of Montford. I cannot read a sermon from the pulpit without stammering, and yet I now have a seat awaiting me in the Lords! Is it not too ludicrous for words?"

"On the contrary, I have long felt that you might benefit from a change of scenery. Although I will confess, I never expected my prayers to be answered in quite so grand a manner. I say, my boy, will you pour? I fear these old hands are not as steady as they once were."

"Of course, sir, but—a change of scenery? Why?"

"Forgive me, but I have often wondered if you might be happier in a place with fewer painful memories."

James became very engrossed in the task of dispensing steaming liquid into two mismatched cups. "I beg you will not think of her. I do not—at least not more than two or three times a day," he added with a humorless laugh.

Mr. Bainbridge did not know the details of his curate's aborted romance, but he knew the young man was as sensitive as any artist or poet, and that his heart, once touched, would not survive the affair unscathed.

"Pray do not refine too much upon it," the old vicar pleaded now. "I do not believe it was her intention to cause you pain."

"No, for to do so she would have to recognize that I had feelings to hurt, would she not? I have no illusions about what I meant to her, Mr. Bainbridge. She wanted someone upon which to practice her charms and, Fairford offering nothing more promising in the way of unattached gentlemen, she set her sights on me. When I made her an offer of marriage, she was much shocked to discover that I took her seeming partiality seriously! Depend upon it, she is much happier in London, where I daresay she has captivated half the peerage by now."

"And yet, if you were to follow her to London and ask her again, you might receive a very different answer," observed the older man, stirring milk into his tea.

"Perhaps," James said slowly. "And yet I wonder if I could be content to wed a lady who I knew accepted me only because of the change in my circumstances."

However much his sympathies lay with his curate, Mr. Bainbridge could not allow one of his parishioners to malign another. "In all fairness, James, you must allow that security is important to a woman, and marriage is the only way that most may achieve it. Do her the justice of owning that it was not a life of ease you offered her."

"I do own it. And if security is what she wants, I hope she may find it. But," he added, "she'll not have it from me."

Within a se'ennight, all James's worldly goods (which consisted, for the most part, of two changes of clothes, a slightly battered violin, and a small but cherished collection of books, most of them purchased at secondhand) were packed into an ancient portmanteau. This, along with James himself, was deposited in the squire's own gig and borne with great ceremony to the Pig and Whistle, from which hostelry the new duke might hire four high-stepping horses and a post-chaise in which to descend upon Montford in a manner befitting his station. Twenty-seven years of frugal living, however, were not so easily set aside. His Grace took the stage.

The two-day journey from Fairford to Montford was not an unalloyed pleasure, as James was obliged to spend hours at a stretch on a poorly padded seat, squeezed between a large woman holding on her lap a howling toddler, and a farmer who whiled away the tedium of the journey by chewing on a particularly odoriferous cheese. James's own attempts to escape the discomforts of his situation via the pages of one of his beloved books were foiled by the loud snores of a stout, red-nosed man in the rear-facing seat. But as James was a sweet-tempered young man (and, perhaps more significantly, had no more pleasurable travels with which to compare it), he bore his sufferings with fortitude. Aside from a slight, sympathetic smile for the stout man's seatmate—who was pressed against the window by his slumbering fellow's girth, and who glowered at James for his pains before returning his gaze to the passing scenery— the duke's feelings were betrayed only by a small sigh of relief when the stagecoach stopped at the Red Lion in Littledean.

But alas, no comfort was to be found within. For here the stout woman discovered to her displeasure that there was no milk to be had for her wailing child.

"What?" she demanded of the landlord. "None at all?"

"None for the stagecoach passengers, any gates," this worthy amended.

"Then who, pray, are you saving it for?" challenged the offended parent.

"The Quality," she was informed roundly. "A fine thing it would be, if they had no milk for their coffee or tea!"

The woman swept a disdainful glance about the taproom, dismissing James and the rest of his fellow passengers with a glance. "I see no Quality here! They patronize better establishments than yours, I trow!"

"Not if they stop in Littledean, they don't, for it has but the one posting-house."

"Hmph! Next you will tell me that Littledean boasts but one cow!"

"Nay, there are at least two, for I'm speaking to one of 'em now," replied the landlord, not without satisfaction.

The woman's face turned purple with rage. "Why, you—" she sputtered. "I ought to—"

"Pardon me, but may I be of some assistance?"

James never raised his voice, but something about his quiet, well-modulated tones had the effect of disarming the combatants, at least for the moment. The woman gestured angrily toward the landlord, who stood with his arms crossed over his apron, glaring back at her.

17

"It's not enough for this monster to starve my poor darling; now he must needs insult me, as well!"

"The mail-coach will be here within the hour," protested the landlord. "How will it look if I can't offer the passengers milk for their coffee or tea, all on account of this woman's mewling brat?"

"Perhaps if the child were fed, he would cease, er, mewling," James suggested reasonably. "Surely a lad his age will not require much."

The landlord's gaze fell ever so briefly, and James, recognizing that a truce was within reach, was emboldened to withdraw from his coat pocket the purse bestowed upon him some days earlier by the solicitor. Spilling its contents into the palm of his hand, he was slightly embarrassed to discover that the pouch contained no coin smaller than a crown. This, however, he did not hesitate to press into the landlord's hand, requesting him to bring the child a cup of milk along with whatever victuals he might have on hand suitable for a child of, James hazarded, four years.

"Three," corrected the child's mother, adding proudly, "But he is a fine, strapping lad for his age, is he not?"

To this James readily agreed. The landlord, looking from the crown piece in his hand to his patron's worn and travel-stained coat, bit the silver coin and, apparently satisfied as to its authenticity, betook himself to the kitchen.

Unbeknownst to James, this exchange had an interested observer in the person of one of his fellow passengers. The wiry little man who had so recently occupied the rear-facing seat watched with interest as James reached for his purse, and as a quantity of gold and silver coins spilled into James's hand, the watcher's eyes could have been seen to gleam. Unobtrusively, he slipped from the taproom and into the yard, where he met the erstwhile slumberer bearing down upon the hostelry carrying a bulging portmanteau under each beefy arm.

"Wait," he commanded this individual, then hailed the coachman. He put a number of questions to this worthy, to which (after a few copper coins exchanged hands) he received satisfactory answers. The stout man with the bags was summoned, and the portmanteaux were returned to the boot.

"But I thought we was stopping in Littledean!" protested the stout man.

"There's been a change of plans," stated his wiry fellow in a voice that brooked no argument.

The journey recommenced a short time later, and it must be stated that this stage passed far more pleasantly than the one which had preceded it. Two of the passengers had disembarked at Littledean and only one newcomer replaced them, to the patent relief of the other travelers. Of those who remained, the stout man, now fully awake, ceased to snore, and the child, his hunger satiated, fell asleep on his mother's bosom. James returned to his book, but was startled and slightly disturbed on two occasions when he glanced up from the page and saw the wiry man in the rear-facing seat staring malevolently in his direction. James quickly dismissed this fanciful notion as the result of reading gothic novels, and resolved that the next time he traveled, he would purchase a newspaper instead.

As the coach neared the village of Montford, it veered unexpectedly around a curve. James, bracing himself in order to avoid tumbling against the mother and child, glanced toward the window, and beheld a vision. Framed against the horizon, a massive brick house built in the Palladian style sat atop a distant hill, its numerous arched windows blindingly reflecting the afternoon sun. Instinctively,

James leaned toward the window for a better view.

Seeing his reaction, the mother shifted the child higher on her lap and bestowed a smug smile upon James. "That's Montford Priory, seat of his Grace, the duke of Montford," she said with all the pride of a native. "It's empty now, so far as I can tell. The old duke died several months back, and we've not yet seen hair nor hide of the new one."

"I hope he proves worthy of such magnificence," James murmured, his eyes never straying from the house until a bend in the road once again hid it from view.

A short time later the coach barreled into the village proper and lurched to a stop before the Pig and Whistle. James disembarked, along with the woman, her sleepy child, and the two men in the rear-facing seat. Having glimpsed his destination, James did not linger inside the posting-house to ask for directions, but collected his belongings and set out for Montford Priory on foot, his portmanteau thumping out a rhythm against his knee with every step.

He had traveled perhaps a quarter of a mile when he realized that he was not the only one of the stagecoach passengers heading in that direction: the wiry little man and his stout companion followed at a distance of some fifty yards. As James could not recall having passed any more likely destinations, he wondered if they too had business at Montford Priory; if so, theirs could only be business of a temporary nature, as they had apparently left their bags at the Pig and Whistle.

Whatever their destination, James observed a few moments later, they were in a remarkable hurry to reach it. The fifty yards between them had quickly closed to a scant twenty feet. As the afternoon sun threw the two men's lengthening shadows across James's path, he looked over

20

his shoulder to speak to his fellow travelers. Before he could make eye contact, however, a beefy fist connected with his jaw, sending him staggering backwards amid an explosion of stars.

Ordinarily, James was blessed with the sweetest of temperaments, but as a scrawny shabby-genteel boy attending school with the sons of England's aristocracy, he had developed a finely honed instinct for self-preservation. Still half-blinded by pain, he nevertheless swung the heavy portmanteau with all his might. A thud and a grunt indicated that he had hit his mark, but a second vicious blow, this one to his nose, robbed him of any satisfaction he might otherwise have derived. Another arc of the portmanteau met only empty air, but the force of James's swing was sufficient to overcome the locks. The ancient bag flew open, disgorging its contents across the road and rendering itself useless as a weapon. He flung it away and balled his fists, but before he had a chance to use them, a blow to his face, swiftly followed by another to his belly, doubled him over, and he fell insensibly to the ground.

"There!" pronounced the larger of his two attackers, dusting off his hands. " 'E 'ad more fight in 'im than I would've thought."

"Never mind that now," said his crony dismissively, rolling his victim's limp form over and plunging a hand into the breast pocket of James's coat. With a grin of satisfaction, he withdrew the coin-filled pouch, along with a sheaf of papers tied with a ribbon. He tossed the purse to his henchman, untied the ribbon, and perused the contents of the packet of letters. One, bearing an impressive red wax seal, caught his attention. He quickly scanned its text, and the words he read there wiped the satisfied smirk from his face.

21

"Bloody hell!" he exclaimed. "We've crowned a blinkin' duke!"

They stuffed their ill-gotten gains into their pockets, then fled the scene as if the Furies were at their heels.

CHAPTER 2

Miss Margaret Darrington, cooling her heels at the Pig and Whistle, tapped a serviceably shod foot and glanced impatiently at the clock over the mantel. The man she had arranged to meet should have arrived on the three o'clock stage, and although Miss Darrington was charitable enough to allow that coaches often fell behind schedule, an hour-long wait had worn her patience (never her strong suit, even under far more sanguine circumstances) quite thin. If Mr. Fanshawe was this unreliable in all matters, then he was clearly unsuitable to have charge over her lively fourteen-year-old brother.

As the hostelry door burst open, Miss Darrington looked up hopefully, only to have her expectations dashed once again. Neither of the two men entering the Pig and Whistle looked at all like a tutor. The larger of the two looked as if he would be more at home at a blacksmith's forge than in a schoolroom, while the other—

Miss Darrington blinked as he looked up at that moment and regarded her with a gaze so malignant that she shuddered, remembering anew the perils that might befall an unaccompanied lady loitering about a public inn. Her mind made up, Miss Darrington strode to the door leading to the stable yard. If Mr. Fanshawe were to arrive at some later time, he could make the five-mile trek to Darrington House on foot. He could while away the tedium of the journey by composing an acceptable excuse for the tardiness of his arrival.

★ ★ ★ ★ ★

Groaning, James sat up in the road and rubbed the sore spot on his head, where a lump was already beginning to form. What had happened? Surely there must be some reason why he was lying here in the middle of the road to—where *did* this road lead, anyway? Turning to survey his surroundings—no easy task, when every muscle in his body screamed in protest—he saw no familiar landmarks, nothing to remind him of where he was or where he had been going.

That he had indeed been going somewhere was evidenced by the open portmanteau lying face-down on the side of the road, clothing strewn about it like a madwoman's laundry. Wincing in pain, he staggered to his feet and began to gather his belongings, now covered with a film of road dust. A single book lay open at his feet, its pages turning in the breeze as if by a ghostly reader. He picked up the volume, and as he blew the dirt from its pages, he saw a name written on the flyleaf: Charles Haslett. James blinked. How very odd that one of his books should bear such a name, when his own name was—

A wave of nausea engulfed him as he realized he could not remember his own name. Panic-stricken, he reached for another book, then another. A dozen volumes yielded almost as many names, each one as unfamiliar as the one before. He fumbled in the breast pocket of his coat for anything that might provide some identification, but came up empty. Who was he, and where was he? Would anyone miss him, and come in search of him? What had happened here? If only he could remember!

"Mr. Fanshawe?"

He had not heard the vehicle's approach, but James started at the sound of its driver's voice as eagerly as a drowning man at the splash of a lifeline. Turning, he saw a gig driven by a lady who appeared less than delighted to see him. He wracked his brain, but found no memory of a brown-haired young lady in her mid-twenties, attractive but not beautiful, whose most striking feature appeared to be a pair of sparkling dark eyes.

"I—do you know me?" James asked, his words somewhat slurred by his rapidly swelling lip.

Transferring the reins to one gauntleted hand, she extended the other to James. "I waited for you at the Pig and Whistle, but I fear we must have missed one another. I am Miss Darrington. It was I who engaged your services," she added, as if this information should explain everything. In fact it explained nothing, but it was reassuring to James to learn that he was not expected to recognize her.

"Pleased to meet you, Miss Darrington," he said, bowing unsteadily over her hand.

The lady's eyebrows descended ominously. "Mr. Fanshawe, are you given to strong drink?"

"Why, no! That is, I—no." James had no recollection of his past habits, but vague memories of other nameless men suffering the aftereffects of that particular vice were enough to convince him that he would not have willingly joined their ranks.

By this time Miss Darrington had had ample time to assimilate James's swollen lip, blackened eye, and blood-encrusted nose. "Good God, Mr. Fanshawe! What has happened to you?"

"Forgive me, Miss Darrington, but I am not myself." In fact, James reflected, he wasn't anyone—at least, not that he could tell. Had the young lady in the gig not come along when she had, he would not even know his own name, much less his destination. "I don't recall exactly what happened, but I must have set out on foot, and been waylaid by ruffians."

"If you set out on foot for Darrington House, the ruffians may have done you a service, for you are headed in quite the wrong direction."

Miss Darrington's mouth was too wide for beauty, but her smile was infectious. James smiled in spite of himself, and winced at the pain in his lip. "At the risk of seeming ungrateful, I could wish they had been gentler in their attempts to set me to rights."

"Oh, dear!" exclaimed Miss Darrington, sliding to one end of the seat so that he might climb up beside her. "Now you think I am laughing at your misfortune! I assure you, nothing could be further from the truth. Only think how shocking it would have been if you had walked all the way to Montford looking the way you do!"

With an effort, James tossed the portmanteau into the gig and climbed up onto the seat. "Do I look that bad?" he asked, exploring the planes of his abused face with a tentative hand.

"You look a positive fright," she replied candidly. "But we shall take you to Darrington House at once, where your injuries may be cleaned and dressed. Then I daresay you will feel much more the thing. You will wish to meet Philip as soon as may be arranged, of course, and I assure you, he will not think the less of you for your adventures."

"Philip?"

"My brother."

This revelation, combined with the Greek and Latin texts he had discovered amongst his scattered possessions, gave James to understand that he had been engaged as tutor to young Philip Darrington.

"And how old is your brother, Miss Darrington?" he

asked, then hastily added, "I'm sure you must have mentioned it in our correspondence, but I fear I don't remember."

"Philip is fourteen," said Miss Darrington, apparently finding nothing to wonder at in this half-truth.

James was slightly taken aback. "Fourteen? I should think he would be at school by now."

"As I told you in my letter, he was always sickly as a child, and so has been privately educated at home."

"And is he to be my only pupil?"

"Yes. With the exception of my brother, we are a household of females. My youngest sister Amanda is eighteen, and will make her come-out next spring. Then there is myself, of course, and my Aunt Hattie—my father's widowed sister, Mrs. Harriet Blaylock. As for staff, we employ a cook, and we have a man who comes up from the village to serve as both groom and gardener. Then there is Tilly, the maid of all work. If you wish, Tilly will launder your linens for two shillings a month or, if you prefer, you may make your own arrangements."

"Thank you, but I shall be happy to give Tilly my custom."

"And so you may tell her very shortly, for here we are."

In proof of these words, she skillfully maneuvered the gig down a narrow lane, at the end of which lay a fine old Tudor dwelling. Though neither large nor particularly elegant, the house was a splendid example of the architecture of its day, and had obviously been well maintained. The half-timbered upper floor boasted diamond-paned windows, while the ancient brick of the lower was partially obscured by a blanket of ivy.

As the gig rolled to a stop before the front door, James stiffly disembarked and turned to hand Miss Darrington down. The effort this simple gesture cost him was not lost on his employer.

"How kind of you, Mr. Fanshawe, when I should be the one assisting you! I can see we shall deal extremely well together."

This last was said with another wide smile as she looked up into the tutor's bruised face. And up. And up. As Miss Darrington was a tall lady, she was not in the habit of tilting her head back when conversing with gentlemen. She found the sensation oddly pleasant. Then she stepped up onto the first of the three stairs leading to the front door, raising her almost to eye level. With the return to more normal proportions, the curious feeling vanished. She supposed she would grow accustomed to it in time.

She opened the door and led him across the paneled entryway and into the drawing room, where a plump lady in a frilled white cap sat knitting before the fire.

"Aunt Hattie, I have returned with Mr. Fanshawe, Philip's new tutor," Miss Darrington announced. "Mr. Fanshawe, my aunt, Mrs. Harriet Blaylock."

"Do call me Aunt Hattie, dear, everyone else does," said Aunt Hattie, her needles clicking together at a rapid pace. "Tell me, Mr. Fanshawe, have you lost a finger?"

The tutor glanced down at his hands, as if this possibility had not occurred to him. "No, Mrs.—Aunt Hattie, all ten appear to be present and accounted for."

"Oh, dear! What a pity," sighed Aunt Hattie, who then hurried to add, "Not a pity for you, of course, for I am sure it must be most unpleasant to lose a finger. But I have lost count of my stitches, and now it appears that this glove will only have four fingers. I thought perhaps if you had lost a finger, I could give this pair to you. One hates to see so much effort go to waste, you know."

"Perhaps the workhouse might know of an eligible, er, four-fingered party," suggested James.

"But of course! What a clever young man you are, to be sure. But then, you must be clever, mustn't you, to be a tutor? Such a good thing, I feel. One is not always so fortunate with governesses. I have known some governesses who appeared to know little more than their pupils."

James said solemnly that he would do his best not to disappoint.

"Oh, I am quite sure you won't," said Aunt Hattie placidly. "I only hope you will not be disappointed in Philip, for he is not at all studious. In fact, he is very much like his father at the same age, and *he,* you know—"

"Aunt Hattie," interrupted Miss Darrington, "have you any wormwood in your medicine basket? Or perhaps some mustard for a plaster?"

"Wormwood, my dear? I don't recall. Why do you ask?"

"Because Mr. Fanshawe is sorely in need of it, along with a quantity of hot water."

Aunt Hattie, having been previously occupied by the condition of the tutor's hands, now fixed her myopic gaze upon his bruised and battered face. "Good heavens! My dear boy, what has happened to you?"

"He erroneously took the road to Montford, and was set upon by footpads."

"Footpads?" echoed Aunt Hattie. "In Montford? Depend upon it, this is what comes of that great house standing empty. First gypsies in the home wood, and now this! In the old duke's day, such a thing would have been unheard of. Footpads, indeed! Although, I must confess, I have often wondered why they are called foot*pads.* The 'foot' part one can understand, since they are not on horseback, like highwaymen, but to my mind, the word 'pad' suggests something soft and gentle, and if you will forgive my saying so, Mr. Fanshawe, you do not look as if they were at all gentle—"

"The wormwood, Aunt Hattie!" urged Margaret.

"Yes, dear." Aunt Hattie rose, laid aside her knitting, and waddled from the room.

She had not been long absent when the door burst open to admit a very young man with the slightly unfinished look of the adolescent who, having reached manhood's height, had yet to attain the corresponding musculature.

"Aunt Hattie says the tutor is here, and that he was set upon by footpads—or highwaymen—or perhaps gypsies? Can't imagine what any of 'em would want with a tutor, but to hear Aunt Hattie tell it—"

"Philip," said his sister, interrupting this burst of eloquence, "you may make your bow to Mr. Fanshawe. As you can see, it is quite true: Mr. Fanshawe met with a mishap on the road."

"Famous!" exclaimed Master Philip Darrington, regarding his instructor with a look of admiration not unmixed with awe. "Oh, how I wish it might have happened to me! Nothing exciting ever does, you know."

James's lips twitched, but he answered with mock solemnity, "I assure you, had I known of your wishes, I should have been happy to give up my place to you."

"Never say you should have wanted to miss such an adventure, for I won't believe you," declared Philip.

"I daresay Mr. Fanshawe thirsts for adventure as much as any other red-blooded Englishman," said Margaret, sponging her employee's injuries with a wet cloth. "Still, one has only to look at him to see that he has had rather too much excitement for his own good."

"In your place, I should have shot them!"

"You will no doubt think it very remiss of me," James confessed, wincing slightly as Miss Darrington touched a tender spot, "but I fear I lacked the foresight to provide myself with pistols."

"Oh," said Philip, manfully concealing his disappointment. "Well, I daresay you hardly expected to happen upon such an adventure. But are you perhaps handy with your fists? Did you draw their cork? Darken their daylights?"

It was a very queer thing, reflected James, that while he could remember nothing of his past life, he had no difficulty in interpreting Master Philip Darrington's store of boxing cant. "Alas, I fear I made a very poor showing," he confessed, fully aware that he was rapidly losing face in his pupil's eyes. Recalling the scattered articles of clothing, he added, "Although I fancy I may have landed a blow or two with my portmanteau, much to its detriment."

"You need not worry about that, at any rate, Mr. Fanshawe," said Margaret, "for I hope you will not be needing your portmanteau anytime soon."

"I should think not!" concurred Philip. "I hope you will be with us for a very long time, Mr. Fanshawe, for it is plain to me that you are a great gun!"

James, having been granted the highest praise of which an adolescent schoolboy was capable, acknowledged this tribute with a slight bow. "I thank you, Master Philip, and only hope you will feel the same when I am excoriating you for neglecting your Latin."

Master Philip received this threat in the manner in which it was intended, and his elder sister, listening to the pair of them, could not but feel that she had been extremely fortunate in finding such a tutor for her lively young brother. The true test, however, still lay ahead, for Mr. Fanshawe

31

had yet to make the acquaintance of Miss Amanda Darrington.

Her self-satisfied smile faded at the prospect.

At the same moment in which the very thought of her erased the smile from her sister's face, Miss Amanda Darrington, all unknowing, descended the path leading from the duke of Montford's orchards to the gurgling stream separating the Darrington property from that of the duke. She made a fetching picture, with a basket of rosy (albeit contraband) apples on her arm and a broad-brimmed straw hat tied with a wide blue ribbon over her golden curls. But Miss Amanda had no thought for her appearance, for her mind was occupied with weightier matters.

Her steps slowed as she began the descent toward the stream, for she wanted to take in every detail of the countryside's autumnal splendor. She might never see it again. With the spring would come her removal to London, and the brilliant marriage it was her duty to make. The prospect, which so consumed her elder sister's waking hours, held no appeal for Amanda. Although she liked new dresses and fine jewels as much as the next damsel, she had lived in Montford all her life, and had no ambitions beyond its borders. To her sister's predictions of her becoming a fine lady, she would have said (had she been allowed to get a word in edgewise) that the only fine lady of her acquaintance was the squire's wife, and if that overbearing female was characteristic of the breed, she would prefer not to join its ranks.

She heaved a sigh, and the small, unhappy sound seemed to be picked up by the air itself, and repeated in the breeze stirring the leaves of the apple trees. How lovely it would be if the new duke of Montford would come and fall in love with her at first sight! He would be young and handsome, of course, and she already knew him to be very rich. They would be married at Christmas, and she would never have to leave Montford. Philip could go to school, and then to University, and Aunt Hattie could have a generous pension, and Margaret could have—whatever it was that Margaret wanted. Amanda was not quite certain, as her sister's ambitions always seemed to center around the other members of the family.

But Life, as she had already discovered, was nothing at all like a fairy tale, and when the duke finally deigned to appear—if he appeared at all, which she was beginning to doubt—he would no doubt be middle-aged and paunchy, with a wife and half a dozen ducal children. No, it appeared she was doomed to London and a brilliant marriage.

Lost in thought, she failed to notice the patch of loose stones until she stepped squarely in the midst of it. The pebbles shifted beneath her feet, briefly upsetting her balance. She was never in danger of falling, but the abrupt movement was sufficient to dislodge one of the apples. It fell to the ground, bounced once, and began to roll down the hill.

"Oh, bother!" muttered Amanda, giving chase.

The apple gained speed as it descended, and Amanda did likewise. How too, too annoying if it should be lost in the stream, when at any moment that disagreeable old *married* duke might appear and put a stop to her clandestine inroads into his apple harvest!

She was breathless by the time she reached the stream, but her efforts had not been in vain. As the apple neared the water, she dropped to her knees and stretched out her arm to snatch at it—just in time to see it roll out of reach and come to a stop against a booted foot.

Amanda, still on her knees, looked up and up, past the shining black leather boot, buff-colored breeches, and brown coat to the wearer's face. At the sight of tightly curling chestnut hair and twinkling hazel eyes, she suffered a shortness of breath and a pounding of heart that had nothing to do with her recent exertions. As the stranger stooped to pick up the apple, she became painfully aware of her disheveled hair and the gypsy hat, once so becoming, now hanging down her back.

"H-have the goodness, sir, to return my property, if you please," she said, finding her tongue at last.

"Your property?" echoed the stranger, offering his hand to help her to her feet. "And who might you be, if I may be so bold? No, don't tell me; let me guess! Demeter, goddess of the harvest! Or do I mean Ceres?"

"As one is Greek and the other Roman, either will suffice, although neither is correct," she said, rising with his assistance and self-consciously brushing the dust from the skirts of her plain round gown.

"Ah! An educated mind as well as a lovely face!"

"You are too kind, sir. Now, if you will return my apple, I will be on my way."

"But as I saved your apple, and quite possibly your own fair self, from a wetting, surely I am deserving of some reward," protested the gentleman.

In the eighteen years of her existence, Amanda had formed a very fair idea of the form such "rewards" generally took. She lifted her chin, puckered her lips, and closed her eyes, her manner reminiscent of a vestal virgin about to be sacrificed to a pagan deity.

"Delicious!" declared the stranger in a muffled voice.

Amanda's eyes flew open just in time to see him sink his teeth for the second time into the apple's crisp, juicy flesh.

For reasons she could not fully explain, she found his taking liberties with her apple even more offensive than the prospect of his taking them with her person. "Release that apple, sir! It is mine!"

"Is it, indeed? I was under the impression that these orchards belonged to the duke of Montford. Unless, of course, you are the duchess?"

A half-formed hope that this handsome stranger might prove to be the duke himself now shriveled and died. "The old duke always allowed me to pick his apples."

"But the old duke is dead. Long live the new one," added the stranger, biting into the apple once again.

"And what right, pray, have *you* to be here?" challenged Amanda, her eyes narrowing in suspicion. "Unless, of course, you are the duke?"

"Alas, I am only Mr. Peregrine Palmer, a mere nobody, at your service," he said, clicking his heels together and sketching a bow.

"Then you have no more right to be here than I do!"

"In fact, I have considerably less," he admitted. "I never knew the old duke, you see. In fact, I have no claim at all save for the demands of an empty belly and a stream full of trout."

"You are poaching the duke's fish!" exclaimed Amanda, noticing for the first time the fishing rod lying on the grassy bank beside the stream.

"Shh!" Mr. Peregrine Palmer put a finger to his lips. "Let's not tell him, shall we? After all, his Grace can hardly miss what he never had."

A broad wink accompanied these words, and Amanda, blushing rosily, gave a little huff of annoyance. "Very well, sir, since you will not return my apple—and I would not have it in its present condition in any case," she added

35

quickly, as he silently offered her the half-eaten core, "I will bid you good day."

As she nimbly picked her way across the stream on strategically placed stones, Mr. Palmer was at last moved to repentance. "I say, don't leave! I meant no offense, Miss—Demeter—wait! I don't even know your name!"

He followed her across the steppingstones, but as he lacked her long acquaintance with them, he made an awkward business of it.

"Please wait, Demeter—"

As she reached the opposite bank, he grabbed at her sleeve, but she snatched her arm away. Resisting the urge to turn around, she heard a swift intake of breath and a muttered oath, then a large splash. Not knowing whether to laugh or cry, she hitched up her skirts and ran up the hill toward home.

CHAPTER 3

By the time she reached her home, Amanda Darrington had worked herself into a high dudgeon. Never in all her eighteen years had she been treated so cavalierly by a man, and it galled her to think that such treatment should come at the hands of one who was not only male, but young and handsome into the bargain. To add insult to injury, the most crushing rejoinders now sprang readily to her lips— now, when it was too late to use them. She hoped she never saw the insufferable fellow again, and wished she knew more about him and where he was staying—only so that she might make a special point of avoiding him, of course.

On this thought, she entered the drawing room and found it in a state of chaos. A fair-haired, bespectacled stranger sat on a straight chair before the fire, with Philip kneeling on the floor at his feet peppering him with questions. Behind him fluttered Aunt Hattie, wringing her hands and making little clucking noises indicative of sympathy. Margaret, wrapping a length of gauze about the stranger's forehead, paused in this endeavor long enough to address her sister in scolding tones.

"Whatever took you so long, Amanda? I was beginning to think—good heavens!" she cried, taking a closer look at her younger sister. "Whatever will Mr. Fanshawe think of you?"

The tutor, however, showed no signs of being repelled by the younger Miss Darrington's appearance. In fact, his open mouth and slightly glazed eyes gave Margaret to understand that he scarcely noticed Amanda's disordered curls and dusty skirt, being fully occupied in assimilating the myriad charms of flashing eyes, flushed cheeks, and swelling bosom.

"Dea certe!" he breathed aloud, to no one in particular.

"Hardly a goddess, Mr. Fanshawe," retorted Miss Darrington with some asperity. "Amanda, this is Philip's new tutor. Mr. Fanshawe, my sister, Amanda."

"How do you do," said Amanda, bobbing the obligatory curtsy. "But—forgive me, but what has happened to you? Have you met with an accident?"

"I—I—I—" floundered James.

"Mr. Fanshawe was set upon by ruffians on the road," Margaret translated, seeing that the tutor's own explanation was likely to be a very long time in coming. "But Aunt Hattie has prepared a mustard plaster, and we shall have him set to rights in a trice. Meanwhile, I suppose we had best send for the doctor, and inform Sir Humphrey. He is a Justice of the Peace and the highest-ranking gentleman in the area, barring the duke," she explained for the sufferer's benefit. "Philip, you may saddle up Daisy and—"

"I'll go," put in Amanda. "I have not yet put off my hat." This was not quite true, as the hat still hung down her back by its ribbon.

"I should hate to put Miss Amanda to any trouble—" protested James, finding his tongue at last.

"It is no trouble at all," she assured him hastily. "Surely each of us has a duty to do what we can to see that such ruffians do not go unpunished."

"Very noble of you, Amanda, but you are hardly dressed for riding," Margaret pointed out, frowning.

"I shan't have to ride. It is the merest stroll, if one takes the shortcut across the stream and through the duke's orchard."

Margaret, tying off her bandage, failed to observe the heightened color that accompanied these words. She was concerned at the moment with a greater puzzle. The last thing she wanted was to cast her sister in an even more romantic light by allowing Mr. Fanshawe to see her as an avenging angel. Yet Amanda's absence would allow her an opportunity to drop a word of warning into the tutor's ear.

"Very well, but do not tarry," she said, relenting. "It looks as if we might have rain before nightfall."

"Thank you!" cried Amanda, flying to the door. Remembering her manners, she paused long enough to execute a quick curtsy and a breathless "pleased to meet you" to the tutor before darting out the door, slamming it behind her in her haste.

"There!" pronounced Margaret, laying aside the remaining strip of gauze. "Now that we have patched you up, Mr. Fanshawe, shall I show you the schoolroom while we wait for the doctor? Mr. Fanshawe?"

James, staring vacantly at the door through with Amanda Darrington had disappeared, made no reply.

"Mr. Fanshawe!" Margaret repeated with perhaps more force than was necessary.

"What? Oh, yes! The schoolroom," said James, blinking. "Yes, I should like to see it."

"Very well," she said, suppressing a sigh. "Follow me."

She led the way upstairs to the uppermost floor of the house. As they climbed, James noted the faint but undeniable signs of impoverished gentility. The house had been well built, for the stairs, though not broad, did not creak. The carpet covering them, however, was threadbare in the center of each riser, and the wall hangings, though clean, were faded.

The schoolroom itself was a large room under the eaves, with an uncarpeted floor and a plain deal table positioned beneath the gable windows for optimal lighting—and, not coincidentally, maximum preservation of candles. A scarred bookcase contained texts in Latin and Greek. James, scanning their titles, wondered how it was that he could remember ancient languages quite vividly, yet could not recall where he had been or what he had done the day before.

"—the globes, although I am not at all certain they will do you much good," his employer was saying. "They are the same ones that I used as a girl, and my governess used to complain that they were outdated even then. Now what, pray, have I said to make you laugh?"

James was not laughing, but he could not help but smile at the implication that Miss Darrington's girlhood lay in the dim and distant past. "One would think you had learned geography by studying cave paintings."

"How very unhandsome of you to say so!" retorted Margaret with an answering smile. "I would have you to know that we had progressed to stone tablets by that time!"

"I stand corrected," said James, and although his tone was meekness itself, his blue eyes twinkled behind the lenses of his spectacles. "But, elderly as you obviously are, should you not be hiring tutors for your own children, rather than your siblings?"

"Ah, so now I am not only ancient, but spinsterish into the bargain!" exclaimed Margaret, unoffended. "It was not always so, I assure you. Oh, I never had a Season in London—we never had the funds for that, even when Papa was alive—but I attended several assemblies in Bath, and even had one proposal of marriage."

"Which you rejected."

She nodded. "He was a widower who needed a mother for his five children. I decided that if I were to raise another woman's children, I would rather by far raise my mother's than a stranger's. She died while Philip was still in the nursery, and Aunt Hattie came to care for us, but—well, you've met Aunt Hattie, so you should not find it surprising that much of the responsibility eventually shifted to me."

"And you never had another offer?"

"There is a distinct lack of eligible suitors in Montford," Margaret explained. Then, seeing the laughter fade from his eyes to be replaced with something akin to pity, she hastily added, "Pray do not think me the victim of a blighted romance, Mr. Fanshawe. He was at least twice my age, and his children were perfect hellions. I daresay if we had wed, I should have made the lot of them miserable—and they no doubt would have returned the favor."

He smiled, but whatever reply he might have made was forgotten as his attention was caught by something outside the window. A glimpse of Amanda, thought Margaret with a sinking heart. Mr. Fanshawe's days were surely numbered, which was a great pity, as Philip had apparently taken a liking to him. She felt a surge of annoyance at her sister, which she knew to be wholly irrational. After all, it was not Amanda's fault that her stunning beauty reduced even the most reasonable men to stammering idiocy. Margaret had always tried not to be jealous of her sister, and usually succeeded. Still, she could not help wondering somewhat wistfully what it must be like to have that effect, just once, on a man. She glanced at the tutor, still gazing fixedly out the window, and sighed.

In fact, she had wronged James, for the sight that so captured his attention was not the beauteous Amanda, but the stately brick edifice crowning a distant hill. "What is that?" he asked, moving closer to the window.

Margaret joined him there, and was surprised and somewhat pleased to find no sign of Amanda. "What? Oh, that! That is Montford Priory, the principal seat of the duke of Montford."

"A right regal old pile."

"Indeed it is, both inside and out."

"And over there?" He tapped on the glass, indicating a broken wall of gray stones just visible through the trees.

"All that remains of the original priory, given to the Weatherly family by Henry VIII after the dissolution of the monasteries," Margaret explained.

"Obviously the Church's loss was the duke's gain," James observed. "Don't tell me the ruins aren't haunted, for I won't believe it!"

"Oh, but they are! At least, the locals insist upon it, although no one has ever actually seen any ghostly monk. He is said to appear only to the heir, usually upon his inheriting the title."

"To demand the return of church property, no doubt," suggested James.

"No, for he makes no attempt to harm, or even to frighten—although I daresay he achieves the latter even without putting forth much effort. I believe his intent is not so much to threaten as it is to inspect. He must wonder why the place has stood empty for so many months."

"Empty?"

Margaret nodded. "Ever since the old duke died. It apparently took some time to trace the new one, but the household staff was informed that he had been found, and would be coming soon to claim his inheritance. There has been no sign of him yet, but we live in daily expectation of his arrival."

"Let us hope that his welcome is rather warmer than mine," remarked James, gingerly touching his bandaged forehead.

"Oh, dear!" exclaimed Margaret. "I hope you are referring to your encounter on the road, and not to your present company."

"*Touché*, Miss Darrington," he replied, acknowledging this riposte with a slight bow. "I assure you, I have no cause for complaint. No man ever had more capable or charming nurses than you, your aunt, and—and M-Miss Amanda."

And that, thought Miss Darrington, settled the matter. If the tutor was already so smitten with her sister that he could not speak her name without stammering and blushing, her choices were limited to dismissing him out of hand, or being embarrassingly frank with him. She found herself reluctant to do the former, for she rather liked the new tutor. Being not at all of a tranquil disposition herself, she found his quiet manner calming and his self-deprecating humor appealing. She opted, therefore, for the latter.

"By which, of course, you mean that Aunt Hattie and I are capable, and Amanda is charming," she remarked. "Mr. Fanshawe, I must be frank. You will have noticed that my sister is possessed of an uncommon beauty."

"Since we are being frank with one another, Miss Darrington, I will point out that a man would have to be blind *not* to notice such a thing."

"Quite. Unfortunately, the village and its environs appear to be sadly lacking in blind men."

"Also in men with four fingers, as your aunt has discovered. In fact," he added, his dimples becoming quite pronounced, "I should say Montford is cursed with blooming health."

An answering smile tugged at her lips, but she would not allow herself to be distracted. "I assure you, Mr. Fanshawe, I am quite serious. You are not the first to entertain hopes in that direction, but it will not do. You must not think of her."

His eyebrows rose above the edges of his spectacles. "This is plain speaking, indeed," he remarked, somewhat taken aback.

"Amanda, you see," she continued, "is to make a brilliant marriage."

"Is she, indeed? And who is the fortunate fellow who is to be her husband?"

Margaret's chin rose. "We don't know yet," she said with a trace of defiance in her voice.

"I see," James said slowly.

Margaret received the uncomfortable impression that he saw a great deal too much. "You have seen my sister; can you doubt her ability to attach a wealthy gentleman?"

"No," confessed James. "But—if I may be so bold—given the dearth of eligible suitors in the area, where is she to meet this worthy?"

To his surprise, her direct gaze slid away almost guiltily. "I had thought perhaps—" She picked up a book from the scarred table and began to thumb idly through its pages. "I had thought perhaps she might marry the duke."

"The duke of Montford?" echoed James incredulously, jerking his thumb in the direction of the Palladian mansion on the hill. "The duke that—correct me if I'm wrong—you've never laid eyes on?"

"Even a duke must marry sometime, if he wishes to ensure the succession," she pointed out, as if it were the most reasonable thing in the word to betroth an angel sight unseen to a man merely for the sake of his worldly goods.

"But—but what if he is already married?"

"In that case, she might marry his son. I should think his heir must be a marquess or an earl at least, wouldn't you?"

"And if he should prove—unsuitable—in some other way?"

"I assure you, Mr. Fanshawe, I am not a monster! I should not wish to see my sister wed to a brute, or a half-wit."

"I am relieved to hear it," confessed James, his eyes twinkling behind his spectacles. "Tell me, am I more eligible than a ducal half-wit, or less?"

Margaret might have taken offense at this question, had she not seen that twinkle, and responded in kind. "Oh, decidedly less! There is still the title to consider, you know, to say nothing of the Priory."

"I am chastened, indeed," said James in a decidedly unrepentant voice.

Margaret returned the book to the table with a thump. "But nor would I wish to see her wed to a man who is unable to provide for her. Remember, Mr. Fanshawe, I know to a farthing how much you earn, and even if two people were capable of living frugally on thirty-six pounds per annum, it has been my observation that scholarly gentlemen are not always—practical."

James, absorbing with some difficulty this unflattering estimation of his character, wondered fleetingly if Miss Darrington's father had been a scholarly gentleman. Then he recalled that lady's ready understanding of his Latin exclamation upon seeing the fair Amanda, and was sure of it. Good God, what sort of household had he come to?

"I realize you must think me shockingly mercenary," she

continued, "but what other option is open to a well-bred young lady?"

"If money is a problem," James said slowly, "perhaps one of you might seek suitable employment. I assure you, working for one's bread is not so dire a fate," he added, with a hint of a smile.

Margaret shook her head. "I daresay we might, but it would never do. My sister is an accomplished artist and musician, but no lady in her right mind would hire her as a governess, lest her husband or son succumb to Amanda's beauty. I, on the other hand, might be imminently suited for such a position, but aside from the fact that I dare not leave the running of the household to Aunt Hattie, I suspect that few ladies desire their daughters to be instructed in Latin or Greek."

"Your own parents obviously thought differently," James observed, testing a theory.

"My father," said Margaret, her voice growing wistful. "It appeared for a while that I was to be an only child, so Papa raised me as the son he supposed he would never have."

"I daresay Philip's appearance put your nose quite out of joint," James remarked.

"Oh, indeed!" She smiled at the memory. "I was nine years old at the time, and thought myself very ill-used."

"Aha!" said James, cocking an ear toward the school-room door. "The usurper approaches!"

Loud footsteps clattered up the stairs, and a moment later Philip burst through the door.

"Meg, are you almost finished? Amanda is back with the doctor."

CHAPTER 4

The interview with Miss Darrington gave James much to think about as he lay upon a narrow cot while the doctor poked and prodded at his sorely abused person. It seemed he was in the employ of a family whose handsome Tudor home concealed from the world a dire financial situation, the solution to which seemed to lie in the marriage of the younger daughter to a man—*any* man—of fortune. James reminded himself that this in itself was not necessarily a tragedy; he knew there were women (although he could not have stated the source of this knowledge) who would welcome the opportunity to make such a match. Where he himself fit into the picture was less certain. Apparently he had responded to Miss Darrington's advertisement, and had been engaged at a salary of thirty-six pounds per annum. But where he had come from, and what he had been doing there, remained a mystery.

"If you would turn your head, please," adjured the doctor, deftly unwrapping the Darrington ladies' handiwork so that he might inspect the wound beneath the bandages.

James obeyed, and found himself facing the open wardrobe in which he had stored his meager belongings. These had offered few clues, as there had been no papers nor anything else which might identify him—nothing, in fact, beyond a ragtag collection of secondhand books; a modest assortment of rather cheerless clothing, including a well-worn evening ensemble shiny at the elbows and knees; and a shaving kit somewhat the worse for its adventures—

nothing that might shed any light on the life he had led before he met Miss Darrington in the road.

"Well now, I believe you'll live," pronounced the doctor at last, his nimble fingers replacing the bandage with the ease of long practice. "You won't be very pretty to look at for the next week or so, but you have excellent nurses in the Darrington ladies. If your aches and pains should keep you awake at night, ask Hattie Blaylock for a drop or two of laudanum in a glass of her blackberry cordial."

"Before you go, doctor," said James, sitting upright and steeling himself to ask the question for which he was not at all sure he wanted to know the answer, "I think you should know that I—I can't remember the attack."

"Can't remember?" echoed the doctor, his bushy eyebrows drawing together in consternation. "What, precisely, can you not remember?"

"Any of it. I can't remember the person—or persons—who set upon me, or what I was doing before, or—" There was more, of course, much more, but something held James back from a full confession.

"Oh, I wouldn't worry about it overmuch," the doctor assured him, packing his instruments back into a worn black leather bag. "It's not unusual in cases like this for the mind to shut out events too unpleasant to remember, particularly when a blow to the head is involved. Depend upon it, you'll remember it all in another day or so—and when you do, you may wish you hadn't," he added with a wink.

James smiled weakly at this sally, but privately doubted it. He had no time to ponder the doctor's words, for Philip came up to inform him that Sir Humphrey Palmer, the local Justice of the Peace, had arrived and wanted to question him. Alas, James could contribute little to Sir Humphrey's investigations beyond a somewhat sheepish confession that he could remember nothing of the man or men who had attacked him. (Of their masculinity, at least, he was certain; it was too humiliating to think he might have been so roughly used by a band of females.) Nor could Sir Humphrey enlighten James, for he had passed the scene of the altercation on his way to Darrington House, and had observed no evidence of foul play at all, much less any suspicious characters lurking in the vicinity.

But if James deemed the interview a disappointment, Sir Humphrey Palmer, for his part, considered it a complete waste of time. How, pray, was he to apprehend a person or persons unknown with no names, no descriptions, not even so much as a list of stolen items said persons might have in their possession? Well, what had happened to that young man was a pity, and he wouldn't wish such a fate on his worst enemy, but there was nothing he could do beyond expressing his sympathy; he hadn't a hope in Hades of bringing any miscreants to justice.

Sir Humphrey's sense of ill usage lent speed to his steps, and by the time he reached his own front stoop, he was convinced that there was something havey-cavey about the whole affair. The more he thought on it, the more certain he became that young Mr. Fanshawe was not telling everything he knew. He only hoped the Darringtons—good family, though poor as church mice, and little Amanda Darrington as pretty a piece as he had seen in many a long year—were not nursing a viper in their bosom.

With these dire thoughts as his only companions, it was hardly surprising that he gave short shrift to the fashionably dressed young man with unaccountably damp hair, who greeted his arrival with a cry of, "Uncle! You've been holding out on me! You never told me that angels dwelt among us."

"Angels?" echoed Sir Humphrey, eyeing with disfavor his nephew and heir presumptive. "Faugh! Nonsense!"

"*An* angel, then. One. I met her by the river."

"*By* the river, Peregrine?" echoed Sir Humphrey, scowling at his nephew's wet curls. "Looks to me like you've been *in* the river."

"That, too," confessed Peregrine Palmer with a sheepish grin. "I suppose you could say she knocked me off balance."

"Literally as well as figuratively, it would appear." Sir Humphrey's scowl deepened as his suspicions grew. "Tell me, Peregrine, when did this momentous event take place?"

"This very afternoon." The younger man glanced at the long-case clock in the hall. "Not more than two hours ago."

"I feared as much," growled Sir Humphrey. He tossed his hat and gloves onto a piecrust table beside the door, then stalked across the hall toward his study. "It appears that you have made the acquaintance of Miss Amanda Darrington."

"Amanda," Peregrine breathed reverently, following in Sir Humphrey's wake. "It suits her. Tell me, Uncle, how soon may I make my bow to Miss Darrington?"

Sir Humphrey's bushy eyebrows rose. "I thought you already had."

"Formally, I mean. I want a proper introduction."

"Harrumph!" barked Sir Humphrey, reaching for the brandy decanter on his desk. "Since when have you ever cared a fig for propriety?"

"Since now," declared Peregrine. "I'm serious about this girl, Uncle."

Sir Humphrey filled two glasses, handed one to his nephew, and drank deeply from the other. "Well, you're barking up the wrong tree. Miss Darrington—Miss Margaret Darrington, that is—means for her sister to marry well, and you haven't a feather to fly with—and won't, so long as I'm above ground."

"Which I hope will be a long time, sir," said Peregrine with amused affection. "Still, I am not utterly penniless, you know. I have my maternal grandmother's fortune, and although it is not large, it is more than sufficient for me to support a wife in comfort."

"That's as may be, but is it sufficient to support her sister, brother, and widowed aunt as well? For nothing less will appease Miss Darrington, I assure you."

"Oh-ho!" exclaimed Peregrine. "So the angel is guarded by a dragon, is she?"

"You are mixing your metaphors, dear boy."

Both men looked up at the invasion of their male sanctorum by Lady Palmer, the wife of one and the aunt of the other.

"Angels are not guarded by dragons," continued her ladyship.

"Amanda Darrington is," her husband informed her bluntly. He refilled his glass, only to see his wife gently but firmly remove it from his unresisting fingers and set it well out of reach.

"Nonsense! Hattie Blaylock is more pea-goose than dragon."

"Indeed she is, my dear," Sir Humphrey concurred. "But I was speaking of Miss Amanda's elder sister."

"Margaret? She is hardly a dragon. I only wish she would forget about finding her sister a husband, and concentrate her efforts on finding one of her own."

Peregrine threw up his hands. "Not interested, thank you!"

Lady Palmer gave a most unladylike snort. "And a very

51

good thing, too, for you haven't the sense to appreciate a
good woman! Amanda Darrington is a sweet child, but her
elder sister is worth ten of her—as you men would see, if
you would be guided by your brains, instead of your—"

"Aunt!"

"Martha!"

Shocked horror was writ large on her husband's countenance, and unholy glee on her nephew's.

"Your *eyes*," she insisted. "I was going to say your *eyes!*"

"Of course you were, Aunt," said Peregrine, still grinning. "Now, how soon can you introduce me to the Misses
Darrington?"

"I might have done so this very afternoon," said Sir
Humphrey. "I've only just returned from the Darrington
place."

"Uncle! Is that any way to treat your own flesh and
blood? You might have taken me along!"

"So I might, had you not decided on a dip in the river,"
Sir Humphrey reminded him.

"I trust you found them all well?" asked Lady Palmer in
some concern. "I confess I am at a loss as to why they felt
the need to send for you. Unless—surely Hattie Blaylock
has not—"

"Oh, Mrs. Blaylock is in blooming health, as are her
nieces and nephew. The trouble concerns Master Philip's
new tutor. Seems the fellow had a run-in with a ruffian or
two on the Montford road."

"Tutor?" Peregrine was not at all pleased at the idea of
another man poaching on his preserves. "What is the fellow
like? Young? Handsome?"

"Probably about your own age. As for handsome, well, I
should say that depends on whether Miss Amanda has a
partiality for black eyes and bloody lips."

"That's all right, then," said Peregrine, his brow clearing.

"On the contrary," put in Lady Palmer, "some women relish the rôle of ministering angel."

"That tears it! This tutor fellow must not be allowed to steal a march on me. Aunt, I throw myself upon your good graces. How soon can you arrange an introduction?"

"We see the Darringtons every Sunday at church. I shall introduce you to Miss Amanda after services, and not one moment before," she said, resigning herself to the inevitable. "Although for my part, I should take Miss Darrington."

"Excellent!" declared Peregrine, grinning at his aunt. "You may have Miss Darrington, and I will take Amanda!"

Lady Palmer gave him a withering glare, and departed in a huff.

Dinner with the Darringtons was so pleasant and peaceful a meal that James would have been surprised to know just how controversial was his presence there. Indeed, he might well have been relegated to taking his meals in the schoolroom, had Aunt Hattie not overheard her niece giving the cook instructions to that effect.

"The schoolroom, Margaret?" she echoed in some consternation. "Surely not!"

"Why not, pray?" asked Miss Darrington, a hint of a challenge in her voice.

"You cannot expect poor Mr. Fanshawe to take his meals all alone!"

"If he wishes for company, perhaps Philip could join him," suggested Margaret.

Aunt Hattie, usually the most biddable of females, gave a snort of derision. "Philip has been dining with the family these two years past. He would be highly offended at being treated as if he were back in leading strings—and who could blame him?"

"Perhaps Mr. Fanshawe would not want his company, in any case," Miss Darrington persisted. "After spending his days trying to drum Latin and Greek into Philip's head, he might welcome a quiet evening to himself."

"If that is the case, we will certainly excuse him. But the choice should be his to make."

There was very little that Margaret could say to this argument, at least while the cook was listening with every indication of interest. But as they left the kitchen, she could not resist chiding her aunt.

"I cannot think it wise to allow Mr. Fanshawe to dine with the family, Aunt Hattie."

"Why not, pray? You sound as if you dislike the poor man."

"I don't *dislike* him, precisely," said Margaret, frowning slightly. "But I dislike very much the way he looks at Amanda. Surely you have not forgotten the last tutor—or the stable boy, or the dancing master!"

Aunt Hattie sniffed. "Dancing master, indeed! A very ill-bred fellow, to be sure! I thought so the minute I laid eyes on him."

"Oh, Aunt, how can you?" retorted Margaret, laughing. "When you said at the time that he was the most charming man you had ever met!"

"Yes, well, I always say that any man with that much charm cannot be trusted."

Margaret, who had never heard her aunt express any such sentiment, merely gave her a knowing look.

"Poor Mr. Fanshawe, on the other hand," continued Aunt Hattie, "appears to be every inch the gentleman."

"Given his extraordinary height, that encompasses a great many inches. You must think him very gentlemanly, indeed," observed Margaret, conceding defeat. If her aunt had already designated the tutor "poor Mr. Fanshawe," then no argument on earth would have the power to move her.

And so it was that James arrayed himself in his threadbare evening clothes and took his place at the dining table. He noted with wry amusement that he was placed between Hattie Blaylock and Margaret Darrington, and wondered if he had Miss Darrington to thank for a seating arrangement that put as much distance as possible between himself and the fair Amanda.

Not surprisingly, conversation at first centered upon Sir Humphrey's visit, and speculation as to the likelihood of anyone being arrested for the assault upon James's person. From there it broadened, for James's benefit, to a description of Sir Humphrey's habits, property, and family situation. On the latter subject, Aunt Hattie provided a contribution that perhaps interested the family more than it did their tutor.

"The vicar's wife informs me that Sir Humphrey's nephew has come down from London for a visit," she said over the fricassee of veal.

Amanda looked up sharply, but Aunt Hattie continued, unnoticing.

"I believe Sir Humphrey and Lady Palmer are much attached to the young man, although Sir Humphrey says he is a rackety sort of fellow."

James smiled at this description. "One wonders how he would have characterized a nephew for whom he felt no affection at all."

"Oh, that is just Sir Humphrey's way," Aunt Hattie assured him. "Surely there must be a great deal of good in a young man who would spend his time visiting his aunt and uncle when he might be enjoying the delights of London."

Amanda, unconvinced, took exception to this assessment. "If he is so devoted, why have we seen no sign of him before now? Depend upon it, he is nothing more than a worthless town-beau, devoted to nothing but his own pleasures. I daresay he came to Montford for no other purpose than to sponge off Sir Humphrey while hiding from his creditors."

This scathing denunciation of an apparent stranger caused Margaret's eyebrows to draw together in a worried crease. What sort of deep game was her sister playing? If this was Amanda's attempt to demonstrate for the tutor's benefit her lack of interest in a life of fashionable frivolity, it was possible that his interest in her was not entirely unreciprocated.

"Oh, dear, do you think so?" fretted Aunt Hattie. "I feel sure you must be mistaken. While it is true that the conduct of the doctor's eldest son while *he* was in London might have been calculated to break his poor father's heart, one must own that he was a sadly ramshackle sort even as a boy— plucking tail feathers from Lady Palmer's peacocks, stealing apples from the duke's orchards—" She shook her head over the youthful sins of the doctor's eldest son, having unwittingly reduced her youngest niece to chastened silence.

Margaret, however, noted her sister's guilty expression, and correctly interpreted it. "Have you been making free with the duke's apples? Really, Amanda, you must not!"

"But he said I might!" Amanda protested.

"The old duke said so, but you have never met the new one, and *he*, you know, may feel quite differently on the subject."

James, beholding his goddess's discomfiture, came swiftly to her rescue. "The duke's orchards," he said. "Might those be the ones I glimpsed from the window of my bedchamber? We must have driven past them on the way, but I fear my impressions are somewhat hazy."

"And no wonder! But yes, the orchards may indeed be seen from the westward-facing windows. If the fine weather holds, perhaps Philip might show you about the place tomorrow after his lessons."

"Or even," put in Philip, "*instead of* his lessons."

James grinned. "Your generosity overwhelms me, Philip, but afterwards will allow us sufficient time, I'm sure."

And, he added mentally, allow him an opportunity to look about him for any clues as to his past or, for that matter, his present.

In this unexceptionable manner, the remainder of the meal passed. The ladies did not withdraw from the table, as Philip was too young to indulge in after-dinner port, and apparently even Aunt Hattie felt that it would be too great a familiarity to allow the tutor to enjoy in solitary splendor the fruit of her late brother's cellars. Instead, the entire company forsook the dining room in favor of a small but comfortably furnished withdrawing room situated at the rear of the house.

James, settling his long frame on one end of a worn horsehair sofa, took stock of his surroundings. A framed watercolor painting of the Darrington family home held pride of place over the mantel, while on an adjacent wall hung a charcoal sketch of a young boy whom he had no difficulty identifying as his pupil.

"You have an artist in the family," he observed, moving nearer for a closer look at the sketch.

"Yes, our Amanda is very talented," agreed Aunt Hattie

57

proudly. "That portrait of Philip is very like, is it not?"

"As well it should be," grumbled Philip. "She forced me to sit on the most uncomfortable chair in the house, and wouldn't let me move for hours!"

"I did no such thing!" protested Amanda. "It was twenty minutes at the very most."

"Hours," reiterated Philip emphatically. "So if she suggests taking down your likeness, you would do well to heed my advice. *Run!"*

"I shall bear it in mind—although I fear my appearance at the moment is hardly a fit subject for any artist."

Her muse now fully awakened, Amanda studied her prospective subject with interest. "No, but I could paint you *en silhouette,* and the bruises would not show. I think you would look very well in profile, for your nose has great character."

"It certainly has great *something,*" conceded James, rubbing his rather prominent proboscis. There arose in his fickle memory a vivid image of himself as a skinny schoolboy, being teased by familiar yet nameless tormentors. "It was a great trial to me in my younger days. As I recall, 'Weathervane' was the nickname of choice."

Amanda wrinkled her *retroussé* little nose. "Schoolboys can be perfectly beastly! I daresay once your bruises have faded, you will look quite distinguished. Do say you will let me take down your silhouette; I assure you, it will not take long, no matter what Philip may say!"

The smile accompanying this appeal was almost blinding in its brilliance. James was not proof against such persuasion. With much stammering and many protestations of his own unworthiness, he at last abandoned the unequal struggle, and agreed to sit for Miss Amanda.

It was a very merry group that set about rearranging the

room. The artist, her eyes sparkling in anticipation, busied herself in stretching a sheet of thin paper across a vertical wooden frame, while Aunt Hattie and Philip debated the best placement of a lamp for throwing the shadow of Mr. Fanshawe's distinctive profile onto the makeshift canvas. As for Mr. Fanshawe himself, he had little to do but sit where he was instructed and follow the often-contradictory advice of the various Darringtons.

The only person who did not seem to enjoy the proceedings was the eldest of the three siblings, who watched with a thoughtful frown creasing her forehead. Long experience had taught her that Amanda was at her most fetching when in the grip of her muse, but the bedazzled tutor, unfamiliar with her sister's idiosyncrasies, might well mistake her animation as a sign of partiality. She took what comfort she could in the realization that these were hardly the ideal circumstances under which to conduct a courtship, as James's infrequent attempts at conversation were met with scolding reminders that he must remain perfectly still.

Alas, even this small comfort was short-lived. At last Amanda laid aside her brush and pronounced her creation finished.

"There you are, Mr. Fanshawe," she declared, removing the paper from its frame and surrendering the painting to its subject for his inspection. "And quite distinguished, too, as I predicted."

Thus dismissed, James rose somewhat stiffly from his seat. "I fear any credit must go to the artist, rather than the subject."

Amanda turned quite pink with pleasure. "You are too kind, Mr. Fanshawe. Handle it carefully, for the paint is still quite wet in the middle, and may smear."

In fact, it had already done so, for a streak of black paint now adorned the corner of Amanda's mouth. The effect should have been ridiculous, but Margaret acknowledged that it was all too likely to inspire a susceptible male with a sudden urge to kiss it away.

"It's lovely, Miss Amanda," James said, although in fact he was not looking at the silhouette at all, but at the dab of paint on her cheek, and his thoughts were running along lines very similar to those imagined by Margaret. "May I keep it?"

"Of course you may! And someday, when Philip is quite grown up and no longer requires your services, you can look at it and remember your time with us."

James regarded it with awe and wonder. "I shall treasure it forever."

Margaret turned away from this touching scene with a sinking heart. For all the good her frank speaking had done, she might as well have saved her breath.

CHAPTER 5

The weather was indeed fine the following day, with a gusty breeze that hinted at the approaching autumn. At half past two, James and his pupil laid aside their Greek and Latin texts and set out to explore the neighborhood on foot, pausing on their way downstairs to invite the ladies of the household to join them. Aunt Hattie declined, citing an earlier promise to assist Cook in preserving the last of the summer peaches, and so James turned his attention to Margaret, laboring at a massive mahogany desk in the room that had once been her father's study.

Margaret was not quite certain why she succumbed, when there were accounts to be paid and ledgers to be balanced. To be sure, it could not have been Mr. Fanshawe's *beaux yeux*—not when one of his eyes was swollen almost shut and beginning to turn an interesting shade of purple. Still, there was something uncommonly persuasive about a gentleman who urged one to abandon one's chores and come with him, just as if it were his dearest wish to spend the rest of the afternoon basking in one's presence. It was not true, of course; any such sentiments on his part were undoubtedly reserved for Amanda, who was already hurrying upstairs to fetch her bonnet. Still, whatever the reason, Margaret found herself laying aside her quill and following her sister up the stairs.

It was Margaret's intention that, in deference to the tutor's injuries, they should limit their ramblings to the Darrington property, merely pointing out those parts of the duke's lands that might be seen in the distance. However, upon James's discovery that mild exercise, rather than exacerbating the soreness of his limbs, actually served to ease their stiffness, he suggested they venture rather farther afield, perhaps as far as the ruins of the ancient monastery. He was gratified to hear Philip and Amanda add their own entreaties, and even more so when Margaret consented to this plan. James could not have said what it was about the sprawling ducal estate that drew him so, especially when he could not recall ever having met or even heard of the duke of Montford, but he could not shake the feeling that the place held some significance for him.

"Tell me, Miss Darrington," he said as they crossed the brook, eschewing Amanda's stepping-stones in favor of the footbridge farther upstream. "Did the old duke leave any children? Young boys, that is, who might have need of a tutor?"

Margaret raised a quizzical eyebrow. "Are you by any chance searching for greener pastures, Mr. Fanshawe? I fear you won't find them at Montford. The old duke left no children, male or female, which accounts for the long delay in locating the new duke."

James merely nodded, and dismissed a promising but unlikely theory. Once over the bridge, the foursome skirted the orchard, where Philip had to be restrained from shinning up a tree and helping himself to contraband fruit. Finally they reached a stile spanning a gap in the hedgerow.

James, assisting first Amanda and then Margaret over the stile, found it surprising that the duke would bisect his own holdings with hedges, and said so. "I should have thought the stream would form a more natural barrier."

"And so it does now," Margaret conceded in a curiously stiff tone. "But the stream did not always mark the property line."

James found this statement perplexing. "The stream meandered, or perhaps its course was deliberately altered?"

"No. The property between the hedges and the stream was not always part of the duke's holdings."

"What she means," explained Philip, leaping from the highest rung and landing lightly on his feet, "is that the orchards once belonged to our family. Papa—or was it Grandpapa?—sold those acres to the duke years ago. Meg says we Darringtons have always been land-rich and cash-poor, only by this time we've sold off so many acres that now we're just plain poor."

"Philip," was all Margaret said, but her voice held a note of warning.

"I see," murmured James, after the younger members of the party had run ahead in pursuit of a brightly colored butterfly.

"If you have any fears regarding your salary, you need not," Margaret hastened to assure him. "I made quite certain of our ability to pay before I engaged your services."

James took her hand and tucked it into the crook of his elbow, and they began the grassy descent toward the crumbled walls of the old monastery. "I have no such fears, believe me. I only meant that I see now why Amanda's marriage is of such vital importance. And also," he added with a hint of a smile, "why your siblings feel a certain sense of entitlement where his Grace's apples are concerned."

"I thought perhaps, if Amanda were to marry the duke, he might deed the orchard back to Philip."

"But surely she need not wed the duke for that. I should think any gentleman of fortune who wins Miss Amanda's hand might be willing to purchase the property and return it to the family."

"Yes, and I should do my utmost to insist upon it as part

of any marriage settlement—provided, of course, that his Grace was willing to sell. Perhaps he might be persuaded to do so as a favor to the bridal pair."

"You would have made a formidable solicitor, Miss Darrington," said James, his smile rendered crooked due to the swelling in his face. "The truth comes out at last!"

"The truth?" echoed Margaret, puzzled. "What truth?"

"The real reason for your single state. You claim a lack of suitors, but in fact, Miss Darrington, you drove too hard a bargain."

"*Touché*, Mr. Fanshawe. In fact, even had there been offers, I must have been obliged to decline them. I fear I should not make anyone a very good wife."

"No? Why not, pray?"

"My dear Mr. Fanshawe, only consider! I have been accustomed to administering the estate for these five years and more, and if it has not precisely prospered, at least I have contrived to keep the house and its remaining grounds off the auction block. Were I to marry, I should no doubt attempt to manage my husband's property. What gentleman would wish to saddle himself with so controlling a female?"

"I should think any man of property would be grateful to have the benefit of his wife's expertise."

She laughed. "If you truly think so, I can only say that your experience of the male sex has been vastly different from—oh!"

She broke off abruptly as a gust of wind tugged the bonnet from her head and sent it tumbling across the grass in the direction of the ancient ruins. James gave chase, his coattails flapping behind him, as Margaret called out encouragement. Once he almost grasped it by its fluttering ribbons, but a fickle breeze snatched the long strips of grosgrain from his reach. Sore muscles screaming in protest, he plunged down the hill toward the crumbling piles of gray stone. Here the bonnet was at last halted in its flight by one of the more intact remnants, a long section of wall about seven feet high.

"*There* you are!" he muttered aloud to the mutinous millinery.

Its ribbons fluttered on the grass as if poised to resume flight. James stooped to pick it up, then turned and blinked in surprise. A short, stout man with the dark robe and tonsured head of a medieval monk stood in the shadow of the wall about thirty feet away, regarding him with an expression of mild curiosity.

"Oh! Good afternoon," James said.

The man made no reply, but turned and walked away, rounding the corner at the end of the broken wall.

"I say—I beg your pardon," James began, but halted in mid-stride at the end of the wall. There was no one there. No one, that is, but Philip, coming around the corner.

"Mr. Fanshawe? Were you calling me?"

"No, I was speaking to the other fellow, but he apparently has no desire for company."

"What other fellow?"

James gestured toward the end of the wall. "The man in the long robe. Surely you saw him? He must have come right past you."

Philip shook his head. "I've seen no one. Unless—" he added, his eyes growing wide with awe. "Never say you've seen the ghost!"

"In broad daylight? Nonsense!" put in Margaret, lifting her skirts so that she might pick her way between the fallen stones. "Besides, only the dukes of Montford may see him."

"Perhaps the ghost mistook Mr. Fanshawe for one of the

Weatherlys," Philip insisted, reluctant to deprive his tutor of so thrilling an experience.

Unlikely though it was, something in the boy's suggestion stirred a chord of memory, and James looked up sharply. Before he could catch hold of it, however, Margaret spoke, and whatever he had almost remembered was gone.

"If that is the case, then he must be a ghost with remarkably poor vision, for Mr. Fanshawe is quite fair, and the duke's people have always been dark."

"On the contrary, Miss Darrington," James said in a flippant tone that belied his unnerving experience. "It would be a perfectly natural mistake. I have always felt there is nothing quite like a black eye and a fat lip for lending a fellow a certain aristocratic air."

Margaret acknowledged this sally with a smile, but declined to answer it with one of her own. "In all seriousness, Mr. Fanshawe, I believe there are gypsies camped in the home wood; no doubt the person you saw was one of them."

"Gypsies!" Having captured the elusive butterfly, Amanda now joined the party with her prize clasped loosely in her hands. "Oh, Meg, do let us have our fortunes told!"

Philip added his entreaties to his sister's. James, for his part, had no great confidence in the purported psychic abilities of gypsies, but as he had had little enough success in ascertaining anything about himself, he reasoned that they could hardly do worse than he had thus far done.

"What say you, Miss Darrington?" he asked with a hint of a challenge in his voice. "Shall we visit the gypsies and put our fates to the test?"

"Yes, let's," she agreed readily, taking his proffered arm. "So long as we return home in time for tea, else Aunt Hattie will worry."

His smile was somewhat sheepish. "I confess, Miss Darrington, you have taken the wind out of my sails. I felt sure you would consider such frivolity a shocking waste of funds."

"And so it is." The twinkle in her fine dark eyes robbed the words of any severity. "But surely everyone deserves an occasional flight of fancy. It has been my observation that harsh reality inevitably rears its ugly head."

It struck James that Miss Darrington had not known enough frivolity in her life. Was she practical by nature, as he had first thought, or had she been forced by circumstances to become so?

As if she had read his thoughts, she added, "Besides, I suspect a close look at the camp will disabuse Amanda and Philip of any romantic notions about the nomadic life."

In this assessment she was almost too correct. Seen at close range, the colorful canvas tents of the gypsies appeared grimy and faded. Two gaunt hounds of mixed breed snarled at their approach. The dogs' animosity was reflected in the hostile stares of a trio of unkempt young men, one of whom poked at the smoldering embers of the campfire with a stout stick.

"What d'ye want?" was this individual's unpromising greeting.

James suddenly found both his arms seized—the left by his employer, and the right by her sister. Glancing first at Miss Darrington, then at Amanda, he saw the two very different young ladies regarding the gypsies with identical expressions of trepidation.

"I—Good day." Seeing the dauntless Miss Darrington for once bereft of speech, James assumed the rôle of spokesman for the group. "The ladies would like to have their fortunes told, if you please."

Apparently the gypsies did not please, for they stared at the group for a long moment before making any attempt to accommodate them. At last one of the young men spat on the ground, then bellowed some strange words in a language James did not understand. Immediately the flap of one of the tents was thrown back, and an elderly woman appeared in the aperture. Her olive skin was deeply lined, but her black hair was scarcely touched with gray in spite of her advanced age. She held a brief discourse with the young man in the unknown tongue, then turned to address the newcomers in heavily accented English.

"You come in."

James did as he was told, steering the Darrington siblings in the direction of the tent and stooping to lead the way through the opening. The abrupt change from sun to shadows made him blink. The interior was too dimly lit to make out much detail, but this might be a good thing, if the smell that assailed his nostrils was anything to judge by. The gypsy crone settled herself on a stool behind a low table covered with a threadbare cloth, then shuffled a deck of cards with surprisingly nimble fingers. Having mixed the cards to her satisfaction, she laid them out face down on the table in a geometric pattern.

"You." She spoke to Amanda, who clung to James's arm in a manner he would have found highly gratifying, had their circumstances been more conducive to romance. "I tell your fortune first."

With the agility of long practice, she turned the cards up, revealing not the simple black and red pips seen in parlor games, but highly detailed scenes featuring elaborate configurations of swords, coins, batons, or cups.

"Ah!" The old gypsy woman grinned, exposing the gaps where several teeth were missing. "Two of cups, six of cups, ten of coins—good, good! You have good and loving husband, much money, and many children. Is very good, no?"

"Oh, very good indeed!" exclaimed Amanda, letting out her breath on a sigh of relief. "See, Meg? I told you everything would come about in the end."

"Amanda, love, one has only to look at you to predict such an outcome," chided Margaret in an undervoice, while the gypsy crone prophesied for Philip a future of travel, wealth, and adventure. "You would be wise not to set too much store by her predictions, however felicitous you may find them. I daresay she tells everyone the same thing, for who would pay good money only to be told of poverty, or illness, or spinsterhood? Depend upon it, she will predict a brilliant marriage for me as well, and assure Mr. Fanshawe that he will inherit a fortune or some such thing."

It was not to be expected that any lively young lady would allow such a statement to go uncontested, and Amanda was more than equal to the challenge.

"I won't believe it! Do let the gypsy tell your fortune next, Mr. Fanshawe, and prove my sister wrong," she urged, tugging at his sleeve.

"Yes, do, Mr. Fanshawe," agreed Margaret, tongue firmly in cheek. "By all means, let us see what delights await you."

Philip was quick to add his entreaties to those of his sisters, and James, seeing all three Darrington siblings allied against him, submitted meekly to his fate. The seer stacked and reshuffled the cards, then dealt them out in the now-familiar pattern and turned them up one by one.

"Interesting," she muttered aloud, after studying the cards in silence for a long moment. "Most interesting. Three of swords—you have suffered a broken heart, yes?"

She pointed to a card picturing a red heart pierced with three swords.

James shrugged, shifting his weight awkwardly from one foot to the other. "Yes, well, who among us has lived for twenty-seven years on this earth without being disappointed in love at some time or another?"

The old gypsy woman nodded. "True, very true. But the other cards say your luck will change. Soon, very soon, you have love—yes, true love and wealth beyond your wildest dreams."

Margaret leaned closer to Amanda to whisper in her ear. "I told you so."

"And now we shall see what lies in store for the other young lady, yes?"

Margaret, finding three pairs of eyes fixed expectantly upon her, lifted her chin. "Very well. What, pray, does my future hold? A handsome and wealthy husband, I daresay."

But the cards beneath the gypsy woman's hand revealed a series of increasingly grim-looking pictures: a man in medieval robes struggling to balance two large coins; a woman, similarly garbed, standing blindfolded and bound amidst eight upright swords; and, most ominous of all, a skeleton on horseback, wielding a scythe. The caption beneath identified this last as Death.

"By Jove!" exclaimed Philip with ghoulish zeal. "Are we going to be putting poor Meg to bed with a shovel?"

"No, no," the old woman assured him. To Margaret, she added, "The card does not mean physical death, but change. You have a decision to make soon, one that will change your life."

"For good or ill?" asked Margaret, drawn into this cryptic prophecy in spite of herself.

The gypsy shrugged, causing her tattered shawl to slip

from one shoulder. "Who can say? All depends on you, on the choices you make."

The two younger Darringtons bombarded her with questions, but the old woman would say no more, apart from vague admonitions to choose carefully. At last the Darrington party exchanged the dark closeness of the tent for the bright sunlight beyond its flap and trudged back up the path toward Darrington House. Amanda and Philip indulged in far-fetched speculations as to how and when their predictions would be fulfilled, but Margaret could not join in their merriment. So certain had she been that her own fortune would be no more than a variation on Amanda's, the gypsy crone's unexpected warning troubled her more than she cared to admit. What choice might she be called upon to make, and how might it change her life? The whole thing was absurd, really; she should put it out of her mind at once.

She was still attempting to put this simple plan into action when James fell back to match his steps with hers.

"You are being unusually quiet, Miss Darrington. I hope the gypsy fortuneteller has not upset you."

Margaret responded a bit too brightly. "Of course not! Even if I were to believe in such things—which I most certainly do not!—I may be assured that my life is not in danger. 'The card means change, not physical death,' " she added in a very fair imitation of the gypsy woman. Hmm, a choice that will change my life. What might she have been thinking of, do you suppose?"

"Miss Amanda's marriage to the duke would certainly change your life," suggested James.

"Yes, but one would think such a change would hinge on Amanda's choice, not mine." She gave a short laugh as they reached the front stoop. "Listen to us, analyzing the old gypsy's predictions as if they would actually come to pass. We might as well speculate as to the source of this fortune you are soon to possess—unless, of course, you are to be retained as tutor to all those children Amanda and the duke are to beget."

James laughed off this suggestion, as was obviously expected of him, but his smile faded to a puzzled frown as he recalled that nowhere in the gypsy camp had he seen anyone bearing the slightest resemblance to the tonsured stranger in the priory ruins.

To Peregrine Palmer, sitting up in bed and reluctantly accepting a cup of herbal tea from his aunt's solicitous hands, the world was a capricious and unjust place. He, at least, felt very hardly used by it, for he had not effected an introduction to Miss Amanda Darrington that Sunday past; in fact, he had not left his bed at all. His unseasonable dunking had metamorphosed into a bout of chills and fever from which he was only now, some ten days later, beginning to recover.

"Your uncle bade me give you this," said Lady Palmer, presenting him with the newspaper she had tucked under her arm. "It is several days old, but perhaps it will help to alleviate your boredom."

"Thank you, Aunt," replied Peregrine, idly turning over the pages of the outdated copy of the *Times*, "and please tell my uncle that I hope to give myself the pleasure of partaking of a glass or two of port with him tonight."

"I cannot think it wise of you to indulge too freely in alcoholic beverages," fretted her ladyship. "A cup of broth, perhaps, or some thin gruel—"

"Good God!" exclaimed Peregrine, bolting upright with such force that herbal tea spilled onto the sheets.

"Very well, we shall dispense with the gruel, but I assure you, Cook's broth is quite tasty—"

"Yes, yes," muttered Peregrine, intent upon the newspaper. "That is, no, do not bring me anyone's broth, for I feel sure I should hate it. But this article on page three—has my uncle seen it?"

"I don't know. I daresay he might not, for the account of the Corn Law debates in Parliament put him so much out of temper that he cast the rest of it aside unread, and said I might give it to you." Her eyes narrowed in sudden suspicion. "You are not going to rant at me about the Corn Laws, are you?"

"No, of course not. But this missing duke of yours—I know him, Aunt!"

"What?" Gruel, broth, and the Corn Laws all forgotten, Lady Palmer leaned forward to read the newspaper over his shoulder. "You know where he is?"

"No, how should I? But I know who he is. We were at school together. His name is—was—James Weatherly. We all called him Weathervane, on account of his nose being rather long."

"Then the more fools you," retorted his aunt. "Surely you must know by now that a large nose in a common man may make him an object of ridicule, but in the heir to a dukedom it must be considered a mark of distinction."

"Amongst schoolboys, Aunt, I assure you it would have made no difference. His being the heir to a dukedom, I mean. Not that we knew he was any such thing, for we didn't. What's more, I'll wager he didn't know it, either. The best of good fellows, but shabby-genteel, and quite resigned to the necessity of earning his own bread." He returned to the study of his newspaper. "And it appears he was doing exactly that. Before he succeeded to the title, he was curate of Fairford parish. According to the *Times*, he departed Fairford a se'ennight past, and was believed to be settled in Montford, until his solicitor called upon him there and found that no one had seen hide nor hair of him."

Lady Palmer found this revelation far less intriguing than did her nephew. "Depend upon it, he is in some tavern, squandering his inheritance on wine, women, and song. You rackety young men are all alike!"

"You are fair and far off there, Aunt," protested Peregrine. "I shan't deny having been rackety enough in my own misspent youth, but I cannot allow you to malign James Weatherly in such a manner, for a steadier fellow I never saw. In fact, it was usually he who rescued the rest of us from the consequences of our excesses."

He frowned down at the newspaper on his lap, but Lady Palmer had the impression that it was not the printed page that he saw in his mind's eye.

"What, then, do you suppose has happened to him?" she asked.

"I don't know, but I refuse to believe he's merrily gone a-wenching while half the world wonders where he is." He set the cup down with a decisive clink, swept the newspaper from the counterpane, and threw back the bedclothes.

"Peregrine, what are you doing?" cried his aunt, aghast. "The doctor says—"

"The doctor be hanged! I should have been on my feet three days ago. If some injury has befallen him while I've been lolling in bed sipping broth—good God, it doesn't bear thinking of!"

Heedless of his aunt's protests, he steered her from the room, firmly shutting the door on her objections. Within five minutes, he was dressed, albeit without his usual elegance, in the buckskins and top boots of the country gentleman. After successfully escaping from the house without encountering his aunt, he went 'round to the stables, ordered his horse saddled, and soon set out in the direction of the Pig and Whistle.

The stage from Littledean had just arrived, so he was obliged to wait while the proprietor tended to the needs of the new arrivals. These, it seemed, were many and varied. Peregrine, who could afford the luxury of traveling by private coach, was unfamiliar with the niceties of stagecoach travel, and watched with detached curiosity as passengers were bundled off and on again with scarcely time to answer Nature's call before the coach set out for its next destination. Of those who disembarked at Montford, some demanded to be fed, while others requested a room where they might stay the night, and still others inquired as to directions or local transportation to their final destinations.

The crowd having at last thinned, Peregrine approached the proprietor, a portly fellow engaged in refreshing himself after his labors with a tankard of ale and a pipe from which he puffed rings of blue smoke.

"Tell me," Peregrine addressed this worthy, "do you recall having seen a tall, fair-haired gentleman of about twenty-seven stop here about a se'ennight past?"

The proprietor sucked on the stem of his pipe. "No, can't say as I do," he pronounced at last. "This here's a busy place. Surely ye can't expect a fellow to remember every stranger passing through."

"Oh, but he didn't pass through. He disembarked here." Clearly, some further description was called for, but as Peregrine had not seen his schoolmate in more than five years, he was not certain to what extent, if any, that young man's appearance might have altered. He decided to concentrate on those aspects most likely to remain. "Surely you must have remarked him: gangly, shabbily dressed, perhaps wearing spectacles—oh, and he had a rather pronounced proboscis."

"Eh?"

"A long nose," explained Peregrine.

The proprietor chuckled, setting his large belly bouncing. "You'll find no shortage of long noses in these parts, thanks to their Graces, the dukes of Montford. *Noblesse oblige,* you know."

Peregrine rather thought *droit du seigneur* was the correct term, but as he had not come to debate the intricacies of the French tongue, he allowed the error to pass. "But you do not recall seeing such a man?"

"Oh, I may have done," admitted mine host. "But I can tell you this much: he never stayed the night under my roof, nor took his mutton here neither, and that's God's own truth, for I never forgot a shilling nor the man what gave it to me."

With this Peregrine had to be content. He thanked the proprietor for his help, such as it was, and gave him a coin for his pains, thereby earning, it must be assumed, a permanent place in that man's memory. Strolling back into the yard, he called for his horse. But even has he placed his foot in the stirrup, he recalled having passed Montford Priory. As he recalled, the distance was not great. Was it possible that James, who'd never had tuppence to rub together, had eschewed more expensive transport and set out on foot? Despite his fears, Peregrine had to smile at the idea of the duke of Montford trudging up to his own door like the lowliest vagabond.

Kicking his foot free of the stirrup, he looped the reins about his wrist and set off down the road, leading the horse alongside him. His mount, unaccustomed to this arrangement, whinnied and nudged Peregrine's arm with his muzzle.

"Yes, I may be three kinds of fool," Peregrine informed the animal, "but something is very rotten in the state of Denmark, and I've a mind to find out what."

Unfortunately, he had no very clear idea of how to go about pursuing this worthy goal. Even his present course of retracing his friend's supposed last steps was no more than a vague impulse, as he had not the faintest idea of what he was looking for or what, if anything, he might expect to find.

Still, any activity was better than none, so he led his horse in the direction of Montford Park. Once outside the village, he provided himself with a walking stick in the form of a stout branch, and with this he periodically explored the vegetation lining both sides of the road. If he had feared to find his erstwhile schoolmate's bloody corpse decaying beneath a hedge, he need not have worried. There were no bodies beneath the hedges; in fact, his random pokes with the stick revealed nothing at all for the first half-mile. Then, thrusting the branch yet again into a promising patch of flora, he caught a glimpse of something white peeking between the green leaves. Hope flared in his bosom that here at last was some proof that James Weatherly had indeed passed this way. A monogrammed handkerchief, or some such personal item, would suit his purposes admirably, as it would provide positive identification. He wondered fleetingly if a curate's income would run to monogramming, and dismissed the likelihood with some regret.

At any rate, the state of James's linens proved to be a moot point, as the white object was not a handkerchief at all, but merely a paper—a discarded letter, in all probability, judging from the wax seal, now broken, overlapping one edge. Dismissing it as of no importance, Peregrine removed his stick, allowing the thick vegetation to fall back into place. He had already stepped away from the hedge when some impulse made him turn back and retrieve the abandoned letter from its hiding place.

It was thicker than he had expected, and he realized that it was not a single sheet, as he had supposed, but a sheaf of several papers. The outer sheet was crumpled and smudged with some reddish-brown substance, but still quite legible, as the hedge had protected the ink from the elements. It bore the name and direction of a London solicitor whose name was unfamiliar, but a closer look at the wax seal revealed the insignia to be that of the College of Arms. Hope flared once more. Peregrine unfolded the papers and scanned page after page of such convoluted text as he had not encountered since his days of studying Latin and Greek at Cambridge. Since James's name figured prominently among the closely written lines, he knew he had found what he sought. Any satisfaction this discovery might have brought him was short-lived, however, for the top sheet bore yet another reddish-brown mark, and this one was not smudged at all; it was the perfect oval of a man's thumbprint.

"Good God, James," murmured Peregrine, staring at the bloodstain in growing horror, "what have they done to you?"

CHAPTER 6

Despite the doctor's cheerful predictions, fully a week passed with no sign of James's errant memory. "Mr. Fanshawe" was not certain precisely why, or at what point, he began to question whether he was, in fact, the person whom the Darringtons believed him to be. Perhaps it was because he could find no sign of any letters between himself and Miss Darrington, although she had referred to such a correspondence several times. He might well be mistaken, but he did not think that was the sort of thing a conscientious employee would have thrown away.

Or perhaps it had more to do with the fact that, even after several days of hearing himself addressed as Mr. Fanshawe, he still found himself startled to realize that it was he who was being spoken to. Surely there ought to be some sense of familiarity in a name to which one had supposedly answered for more than a quarter of a century.

But if he was not the tutor Mr. Fanshawe, then who was he and what was he doing in Montford? It was clear that he had no acquaintances here. When he had attended church services with the family on Sunday, not even the vicar (whom he had somehow expected to be much older than the stripling who had made calf-eyes at Amanda throughout his lengthy homily on brotherly love) had seemed to know him.

Still less did he understand his peculiar fascination with the vacant house on the hill. For he could not pass by the schoolroom window without his gaze straying toward the magnificent structure that was Montford Priory. He was fairly certain he had no personal knowledge of it, nor ever been inside its walls, but this conviction required no feat of memory; one had only to inspect his meager wardrobe to know that he was not accustomed to moving in such exalted circles.

"Would you like to see the inside?"

The sound of his pupil's voice jolted James from his reverie. Philip, supposedly hard at work translating a passage from Herodotus, had laid aside his pen and was regarding his tutor fixedly.

"I—I beg your pardon?" stammered James, disconcerted to find himself the object of such close scrutiny.

"Montford Priory. You seem frightfully taken with it."

Frightful was the word, thought James, although he was not sure why. "Surely anyone with an interest in history must find it a fascinating place."

"Would you like to see the inside?" Philip asked again. "You can, you know. With no duke in residence, you might even persuade Mrs. Collins—she's the duke's housekeeper—to show you the public rooms, as well as some of the first-floor rooms upstairs."

"I should not wish to pry," protested James.

"Pry?" scoffed Philip. "His Grace's staff has little enough to do these days. If you ask Mrs. Collins to show you the house, she'll probably fall on your neck. My sister Meg loves the place like it was her own. I daresay she'd be happy to arrange an outing, if you're interested."

"I am, thank you," James said. Perhaps if he saw the place up close he could identify precisely what it was that drew him so strongly. "And now," he added, attempting without success to appear stern, "you have contrived to avoid your Greek quite long enough. I believe Herodotus is about to enlighten us with his theories regarding the flow of the Nile."

Philip looked down at the expanse of paper yet to be filled and threw down his quill, sprinkling fine drops of ink over the pristine white. "What the dev—deuce does it matter?" he muttered, displaying one of the mercurial mood changes so characteristic of adolescents. "Truth to tell, I don't care what his theories are. I'm tired of just reading about things. I want to go places and do things!"

James knew he should chastise Philip for his outburst of temperament, but he could not but feel a certain sympathy for the boy. Surely it was not natural for a lad of fourteen to be confined to a house full of women. "Far be it from me to question your sister's judgment," he said cautiously, "but I should think you would be happier at school."

"Wouldn't I just!"

"Then why—?"

Philip rolled his eyes. "It is the most nonsensical thing! Just because I was sickly as a child, Meg thinks the rigors of public-school life would be fatal to my delicate constitution." The last two words were spoken with such loathing that James understood the argument was an oft-repeated one.

"You look healthy as a horse to me," James observed.

"Try telling my sister that!"

"You know," said James, frowning thoughtfully into space, "I might just do that."

He found her in the small herb garden behind the kitchen, on her knees in the dirt and wielding a trowel with brisk efficiency.

"Miss Darrington, may I have a word with you?"

At the sound of the tutor's voice, the trowel slipped from her hand.

"Mr. Fanshawe!" she exclaimed, suddenly and painfully conscious of her shabbiest frock, its skirts now liberally sprinkled with dirt. "How you startled me!"

"I beg your pardon. Such was not my intention, I assure you."

She pushed her straw hat further back on her head and smiled up at him. "That, at least, must relieve my mind, for to discover otherwise must have given me the oddest notion of your character."

Brushing the dirt from her faded cotton skirts with one gauntleted hand, she made as if to rise, and found her elbow taken in a surprisingly firm grip. She was somewhat taken aback by the ease with which the tutor lifted her to her feet, as nothing in his long and lanky frame was suggestive of great strength. A moment's reflection, however, was sufficient to remind her that, as his wages would hardly allow for the hire of a servant, he must of necessity be accustomed to doing for himself—hauling his own coal, for instance, or chopping his own firewood, or any number of tasks which, with repetition, must serve to build up the muscles in one's limbs. Surely, she reminded herself sternly, strength was not an attribute to be particularly admired when it was gained through poverty. There could be no reason, then, for the frisson of awareness that coursed through her body at his touch.

Now safely on her feet, Margaret stepped back, disengaging her elbow from his grasp. "What did you wish to speak to me about, Mr. Fanshawe? Is my brother neglecting his lessons?"

"You need have no fear of that, Miss Darrington. I

should be more concerned about a lad his age who did *not* neglect them."

"Yes, I see your point. Then what, pray, is the trouble?"

He shook his head, causing one lock of golden hair to droop over his forehead. "No trouble, merely curiosity. It occurred to me that perhaps Philip would be happier in the company of boys his own age. To be blunt, I cannot help wondering why he is not at school."

Margaret, conscious of an irrational urge to brush back the errant lock of hair, stiffened. "Can you not, Mr. Fanshawe? I was quite sure I explained the situation in my letter. A series of childhood illnesses has made it preferable that Philip be educated quietly at home."

"Childhood illnesses?"

She nodded. "An asthmatic complaint."

"But Philip's childhood days are numbered, and I believe such complaints as you describe are often outgrown as the sufferer reaches adulthood. Surely it is time he was sent to school, where he might form the sort of connections imperative to one who must make his own way in the world."

"If you mean, Mr. Fanshawe, that by going to school Philip might someday follow your own example and end by tutoring Latin and Greek for a mere thirty-six pounds per annum, then he should certainly be educated at home." Upon seeing the shocked and, yes, wounded expression that greeted these words, Margaret turned away abruptly and embarked upon a diligent search for her trowel. "I beg your pardon. That was—unkind."

"Brutally frank, perhaps, but undeniably true." James bent to pick up the small shovel, and placed it in her hand.

"Thank you," she murmured, somewhat abashed at finding her own lack of civility answered with undeserved courtesy. Studiously avoiding his gaze, she hitched up her skirts and began to pick her way gingerly through neat beds of fragrant herbs. "Tell me, Mr. Fanshawe, did you approach me at Philip's instigation?"

"No, although he knows I intend to speak to you on the subject. I made him no promises of success, however. Forgive me, but the thought has occurred to me that perhaps your concerns had more to do with economy than health."

She stopped so abruptly that James, following along behind, almost ran into her.

"He truly was sickly as a child, so much so that at times we feared for his life," she said defensively. "That much, I assure you, is no exaggeration. And, lest you think us utterly destitute, I daresay we could scrape together enough for his tuition. But I am well aware of how cruel children can be to those they deem inferior to themselves. I would not wish his lack of fortune to make him a laughingstock."

At these words, a wisp of memory stirred in James's brain, only to vanish when he tried to seize hold of it. Still, the impression that lingered was strong enough to convince him that Miss Darrington's fears for her brother were not entirely unwarranted.

"I see your point—indeed, my own school days would appear to support your case. And yet I survived the ordeal, as have countless others beside. I have no doubt Philip would do the same."

She regarded him quizzically. "Have you considered, Mr. Fanshawe, that were I to follow your advice and enroll Philip in school, you should find yourself without a position?"

"It did cross my mind," confessed James with a rueful smile. "But I should be a very poor mentor to Philip if I were to advance my own interests at the expense of his."

"I might have known you would put me in my place,"

she observed, rolling her eyes.

James, appalled at having his words so grossly misinterpreted, threw up his hands in mock surrender. "I assure you, Miss Darrington, I meant no offense."

"No, I am quite certain you did not—which makes my own conduct all the more deplorable by comparison. Very well, Mr. Fanshawe, I shall bear it in mind—but I make no promises, and so you may tell my brother."

With this James (and, by extension, Philip) had to be content. And yet something changed that day between mistress and employer, something Margaret could not quite put her finger on. By tacit agreement, neither she nor the tutor made any further mention of their disagreement. Still, the incident had quite cut up her peace. She was determined that he would wed Amanda only over her own dead body; however, she was painfully aware that in allowing that determination to override even the barest civility, she was guilty of far greater sins than any he had as yet committed. She thought again of the unexpected thrill of awareness that had coursed through her at his touch, and wondered if the two wholly uncharacteristic responses were somehow related. Whatever the reason, she found it hard to forgive herself for such a lapse in manners, and harder still to forget it.

Perhaps it was for this reason that she had difficulty falling asleep that night. Whatever the cause, she eventually tired of tossing and turning in her bed, and finally gave up the struggle altogether. Throwing back the counterpane, she got up, slipped a faded dressing gown over her night rail, and went downstairs to the room that had once been her father's study. For the next half-hour, she labored over a leather-bound ledger, calculating columns of figures by the light of a single tallow candle until an unexpected sound interrupted her work.

There was nothing inherently frightening in the sound; in fact, it was quite lovely, the sweet, sad notes of a violin playing somewhere near at hand. One of the local lads, perhaps, come to serenade Amanda by moonlight? If so, her sister's swain was singularly inept: not only was the night sky overcast with clouds, but her sister's bedchamber was on quite the opposite end of the house.

Then she remembered the gypsies camped in the duke's home wood, and stiffened at the memory of the rough men gathered around the campfire. If such a ramshackle lot should choose to relieve the Darrington estate of what remained of its livestock, how could three women and a mere boy hope to withstand them? It was at times such as this that she missed having a man's solid presence about the place. She snuffed her candle and moved quietly to the window, then cautiously lifted one corner of the curtains and peered out. A dark form occupied the curved bench encircling a large oak tree, its shape rendered bizarre by the instrument jutting out from the vicinity of its shoulder. Margaret made her way stealthily out of the room and across the hall, pausing only long enough to arm herself with the iron poker from the fireplace before flinging open the door.

"Who—who is it?" she demanded in what she hoped was a firm voice, wielding the poker like a truncheon. "Identify yourself!"

The musician lowered the violin as he stood up, unfolding absurdly long limbs that put Margaret forcibly in mind of the long-legged spiders that populated the stables. At the same moment, the moon broke through the clouds, turning the violinist's golden hair to silver.

She dropped the poker and clasped one shaking hand to

her bosom. "Oh, Mr. Fanshawe, it is only you!"

If James's lips twitched at this unflattering assessment, he gave no other sign of having noticed it at all. "Did my playing disturb you? I beg your pardon; I had thought no one would be able to hear it."

"I daresay I should not, had I been in my bedroom. But I was unable to sleep, so I was in the study working on the accounts."

"At this hour? It is obvious to me, Miss Darrington, that you shoulder too many responsibilities. Have you thought of employing a steward? You will call it an unnecessary expense, I know, but surely any help in lightening the load must be considered money well spent."

She crossed the moonlight-dappled terrace and seated herself beside him on the bench. "My father once hired a steward, as he had no head for figures. When Papa died, Mr. Jarvis suggested that he might be in a better position to look after the Darrington interests were he a member of the family, rather than merely a paid employee."

James cocked his head. "Meaning?"

"He wished to become Amanda's husband. He was fifty years old if he was a day. She was not quite sixteen."

"I begin to see why you are, shall we say, a bit protective where she is concerned." He opened the violin case and began to pack the instrument tenderly away.

"Oh, pray do not stop playing on my account," Margaret protested. "I should enjoy listening to you, now that I have no fear of being murdered in my bed by violin-playing vagrants."

"How shocking that would be!" exclaimed James, much struck. "I have always felt that musically inclined criminals must be the worst kind."

"Very true," Margaret agreed, entering into the spirit of

the thing. "For their music entices one into lowering one's guard."

James gave her a quizzical smile. "Hmm, I wonder if anyone could. Tell me, do you know 'Over the Hills and Far Away?' Do say you will join me!"

Margaret hastily demurred. "You would very quickly regret extending the invitation, I fear. In truth, Mr. Fanshawe, I have a tin ear."

"False modesty, Miss Darrington," he chided, wagging a finger at her. "You forget I sat next to you in church Sunday last. You sing a very pleasing contralto."

"All right then, suffice it to say that my voice is not well suited to solo performance."

"Perhaps you were never meant to sing alone."

Margaret could think of no ready reply. Certainly the words were no compliment to her vocal abilities and yet, left hanging in the night air, they seemed ripe with some unspoken promise. The tutor must have felt it as well, for he cleared his throat, tucked the instrument under his chin, and cleared his throat again.

"Well then, shall we begin?" he said briskly. " 'Were I laid on Greenland's coast, And in my arms embraced my lass . . .' "

He sang in a pleasant light tenor, and Margaret was emboldened to join him on the chorus.

" 'And I would love you all the day, If with me you'd fondly stray, Over the hills and far away.' "

Their voices blended very well, and so pleased were they with this discovery that they launched into the second stanza, with Margaret taking the melody. After repeating the chorus twice, they lapsed once more into silence. A cool breeze rustled the leaves overhead, and Margaret pulled her dressing gown more closely about her throat.

"The summer will soon be gone," she observed. "The nights are already growing cooler."

"Perhaps it is just as well, then, that we are not on Greenland's coast, as the song says."

"True, but I must confess that the prospect of being 'sold on Indian soil' holds even less appeal, however mild the weather. I think I had best take my chances with the Montford winter."

"I suspect it would take a great deal to budge you from your home."

She drew back and regarded him with an expression of some surprise. "Do you indeed? I wonder how you came to conceive such a false impression? No, Mr. Fanshawe, I am well aware that Darrington Place is not mine, but Philip's. Eventually the estate will be turned over to him, and the household to his wife. I have often thought that, when that day comes, it would be very agreeable to have sufficient funds to see a bit more of the world than I have thus far had opportunity."

James sketched a slight bow. "I stand corrected."

"And what of you, Mr. Fanshawe? Have you any desire for travel abroad? I find it hard to believe that one could devote one's life expounding upon the glories of Rome and Greece without wishing to see them just once in person."

"Very true. Alas, a tutor's wages rarely stretch to foreign travel."

"It is a great pity you could not do so with your own tutor, when you were younger. How shabby of Napoleon to ruin the Grand Tour for an entire generation of young men!"

"And even shabbier for your sake that young ladies are denied the opportunity altogether."

"Oh, but I had the advantage of a scholarly father with

progressive ideas. In fact, Mr. Fanshawe, I spent a month in Bath, where I not only danced at the assemblies, but also examined the ancient Roman baths." She chuckled at the memory. "Poor Aunt Hattie! She was much shocked to learn that the Roman men and women had bathed together unclothed, and decided that it was not at all a suitable place for gently bred young ladies."

"I can see why she might feel that way. One might at any moment round the corner onto Milsom Street and find one-self face-to-face with a naked Roman."

Margaret could not help laughing at the image conjured up by this sally, shocking though it was. How very odd, that conversing with a gentleman upon improper topics while *en dishabille* should feel so very comfortable and, yes, so very *right*. The shiver that ran through her might have been caused by the night breeze, or by some other, less readily identifiable source. She crossed her arms, hugging her body for warmth.

"You are chilled," said James, observing this gesture. He put his violin away almost lovingly, and rose to his feet. "I'm a selfish brute to keep you out here, when you should have been in your bed this past hour and more."

"No, no, I am glad we had this time to speak uninterrupted. We—we understand each other better now, I think."

"Indeed we do. Shall we go back inside?"

Margaret agreed, yet it was with an undeniable sense of loss that she allowed James to open the door and usher her into the dark and silent house.

CHAPTER 7

It would have been an exaggeration to say that their meeting at breakfast the following morning was awkward. Still, Margaret was conscious of a heightened awareness where the tutor was concerned, as evidenced by a certain reluctance to look in his direction and a disturbing tendency to blush whenever she ventured a glance at him and found him looking back. Fortunately, the appearance of Aunt Hattie at the breakfast table in her best bonnet and pelisse quickly banished such foolish notions.

"Are you going somewhere, Aunt Hattie?"

"Indeed, I am!" declared that lady with more forcefulness than was her wont. "I am going to speak to Sir Humphrey about these gypsies. Surely there must be something he can do!"

"The gypsies?" echoed Philip around a mouthful of buttered eggs. "Why? What have they done?"

"Oh, I hope Sir Humphrey won't be too hard on them, after the old woman predicted such a lovely fortune for me," Amanda said with a reminiscent sigh. "A handsome husband, beautiful children—"

"Pray do not talk nonsense, Amanda. And Philip, no one is going to take your breakfast away, so you need not wolf it all down in one bite." Having disposed of her siblings, Margaret turned her attention back to her aunt. "Still, Aunt Hattie, Amanda and Philip have a point. I see no harm in them, so long as they keep to themselves—"

"Ah, but that is just what they *don't* do! Last night I

heard them singing quite near at hand—practically beneath my window, I'm sure."

Margaret's arrested gaze flew to James. "Singing, Aunt?" she echoed, her voice trembling with suppressed emotion.

"Yes, and playing fiddles, too. Such a caterwauling you never heard!"

At this unflattering description, the guilty pair's self-control fled. James abandoned a futile attempt at biting his lip and grinned broadly, while Margaret laughed aloud. At length their private joke was interrupted by the realization that the three other persons at the table were staring at them with varying degrees of bewilderment.

"I'm sorry you were frightened, Aunt Hattie," James said ruefully. "I fear Miss Darrington and I are the culprits. I had difficulty falling asleep, and took my violin out onto the terrace. Your niece was kind enough to bear me company. I had no idea you would be able to hear us on the other end of the house."

Aunt Hattie, nonplussed, looked from her niece to the tutor. "Oh. Well, I must say, I thought their voices blended uncommonly well."

James held up a hand to forestall her. "No, no, don't spoil it! You said we were caterwauling, and I have no doubt we were."

Margaret smiled. "If your sleep was disturbed, Aunt, you must blame Mr. Fanshawe. I warned him I was no singer, but he bewitched me with moonlight and violin music." Too late, she realized that these words carried a context she had not intended. She cleared her throat and added briskly, "Yes, well, Philip tells me you are interested in seeing the Priory, Mr. Fanshawe—the new one, that is, since you have already seen the ruin. Shall I send a note 'round to the housekeeper and ask if the two of you may visit this afternoon?"

James readily agreed to this plan, but only under the condition that the ladies join the outing as well. And so it was that, at two o'clock, a party of four set out from Darrington House, Aunt Hattie electing to call on the squire's wife instead. As the Darrington stables did not stretch to mount four persons at once, they were obliged to make the journey on foot, to Philip's quite vocal displeasure.

"I wish we might have ridden instead," he complained as they approached the bridge. "What I wouldn't give for a good gallop!"

"That will do, Philip." The warning note in Margaret's voice gave James to understand that the depletion of the Darrington stables was an oft-repeated complaint.

"Besides," she added in a brighter tone, "you surely cannot expect Mr. Fanshawe to ride poor old Buttercup."

Philip, unchastened, grinned broadly at the thought of his lanky tutor riding the Darrington siblings' old pony. "I should think not! Why, his feet would no doubt drag the ground."

His sisters found the idea equally hilarious, leaving James to smile uncertainly at their laughter.

"We are not mocking you, I promise," Margaret hastened to assure him. "We all of us learned to ride on Buttercup, and although her best days are behind her, we cannot bring ourselves to part with her."

"And besides, who else would have her?" added Philip, sentiment yielding to practicality. "Aside from being long in the tooth, she's grown fat as a flawn in her old age. Still, I'd rather ride even old Buttercup than walk any day."

"Then you are well named," James observed.

"Oh?" asked Philip. "What do you mean?"

"Your name is from the Greek. 'Philip' means 'lover of horses.' "

"I say!" exclaimed Philip, much struck. "Those Greeks may have been right 'uns, after all! What does 'Herodotus' mean?"

" 'Borer of schoolboys'?" suggested Margaret.

James grinned at her, his dimples very much in evidence. "Very likely."

"What about 'Margaret'?" demanded Philip.

"Also Greek. It means 'pearl.' "

Philip hooted with laughter in a manner highly unflattering to his eldest sister. "What about 'Amanda'?"

James's ears turned pink. "Latin. It means 'worthy of love.' "

"It would," muttered Margaret, suddenly weary to the teeth with the childish game.

"Lord, who'd have thought those old Romans were such a mawkish lot?" Philip said scornfully, echoing his sister's sentiments.

Arriving at the Priory, they eschewed the stately front entrance, as they were not invited guests, and presented themselves instead at the kitchen door. Mrs. Collins, the duke's housekeeper, greeted them with cries of delight, expressing her willingness not only to show them through the duke's house, but to ply them with tea and cakes at his Grace's expense as well.

"No, no," Margaret made haste to decline this offer. "I should not wish to impose upon his Grace's hospitality. Mr. Fanshawe, my brother's tutor, merely expressed admiration for the house, as well as a desire for a closer acquaintance with it."

Mrs. Collins, who had been inclined to look askance at James's shabby clothing and unassuming manner, now realized that he was a sensitive and discerning young man who felt just as he ought. "And quite right, too," she said, beaming her approval. "No one can truly say they've been to Montford until they've had a look at the big house, now, can they? You're quite sure you wouldn't care for a cup of tea?"

James, to whom this offer was tendered, echoed Miss Darrington's refusal as firmly as he dared. Mrs. Collins clicked her tongue over this, protesting that heaven only knew Mr. Fanshawe could use some meat on his bones. Eventually she was obliged to surrender with a good grace, and escorted the party to the foyer whence the tour began.

As they made their way through the elaborately furnished rooms on the ground floor, Margaret was moved to compliment Mrs. Collins on the efficiency of her staff.

"Not all servants would be so painstaking, given the extended absence of their new master," she observed, running a gloved finger over the shining surface of an elegant pie-crust table and examining it for traces of dust.

"That's true, more's the pity," nodded Mrs. Collins. "But I never did hold with laziness. Whether the late duke was here or in Timbuktu, it makes no never-mind, as far as I'm concerned."

"Well spoken, Mrs. Collins. I only hope the new duke will realize how fortunate he is."

The housekeeper preened. "As to that, miss, I'm sure it's not my place to say. I just do my poor best, knowing that one day his Grace will turn up, and I'll have no cause to be ashamed."

James, lacking Margaret's familiarity with the house, was less interested in housekeeping than in examining his surroundings. These were certainly impressive, particularly the marble floor laid out in diamond patterns of black and white, and the two suits of fourteenth-century armor flanking a staircase so wide that the entire Darrington party might have walked up it abreast. Mrs. Collins delivered with all the pride of ownership a brief lecture on the room's most significant features, then led the group into what she called the Red Saloon.

The reason for this soubriquet soon became obvious, as James passed through a paneled door into a large square chamber hung with scarlet silk and carpeted with a rich crimson rug of Oriental design. The furnishings here, though less overtly threatening than the medieval armor in the Hall, were nonetheless intimidating by their very elegance. A more knowledgeable eye might have recognized the hand of Robert Adam in the classically inspired carvings adorning the fireplace, but James, knowing little of such things, was more interested in the portrait hanging over the mantel. Depicting a family at the turn of the previous century, it comprised a long-nosed man with elaborately curled and powdered hair, and a haughty, equally long-nosed young man who held his chin at an arrogant angle. The duke and his heir, James judged, as indicated by the father's hand on the shoulder of his son. Between the two men, a rather mousy woman in wide satin skirts and an elaborate coiffure held a small child on her lap and gazed fondly down at her feet, where a dog of indeterminate breed lapped up milk spilled from an overturned pail.

James was not alone in his interest. Amanda moved toward the painting as if drawn by a magnet. "Oh, how lovely! And yet," she temporized on closer inspection, "it looks somehow unfinished, does it not? Perhaps unfinished is the wrong word, but—out of balance, surely?"

"Why is the duchess simpering at that cur?" demanded Philip.

"You've a good eye, both of you, and no mistake," said Mrs. Collins, beaming at both of them in turn. "That's the fourth duke, painted by William Hogarth before he become famous."

"I thought so!" cried Amanda, immensely pleased with herself. "But an early Hogarth? It must be worth a fortune!"

"No, miss, that it's not, and I'll tell you why. Not long after this painting was done, the duke's second son, Lord Robert, up and married a dairymaid."

"Oh, how romantic!" cried Amanda, to her sister's dismay.

"Well now, miss, I'm afraid that's exactly what it was not," Mrs. Collins continued. "The old duke, he was that angry, he cut off poor Lord Robert without a brass farthing, and forbade anyone from so much as mentioning his name. Yes, and then he hired a painter to paint right over Lord Robert's picture."

"But that's criminal!" cried Margaret.

James regarded his employer with new eyes. "Why, Miss Darrington, I had no idea you were such a romantic."

"Oh, bother romance! I find it appalling that a portrait which might have been one of England's great treasures should be vandalized merely for spite."

"I say!" Philip exclaimed, peering more closely at the portrait as if looking for the prodigal son concealed beneath the crudely applied outer layer of paint. "I'll bet the duchess is supposed to be smiling at Lord Robert!"

"Indeed, she is," nodded Mrs. Collins. "Lord Robert was ever her favorite, or so they say. In fact, some claim that it was for her sake that the artist didn't erase every last trace of the lovers as the duke had ordered, but hid them within the painting."

"Where?" demanded Philip. "I don't see them anywhere."

"Of course you do," chided his elder sister. "They are

right in front of you—the dog and the overturned milk pail."

"How very clever of him!" exclaimed Amanda, examining the portrait with renewed interest. "He may not have Hogarth's talent, but surely his use of symbolism cannot be faulted. Pray, what happened to them? Lord Robert and his bride, I mean."

"No one knows for sure," the housekeeper informed her enthralled audience. "His Grace banished the pair of them from Montford, and they were never seen nor heard from again."

"It must have been quite a shock to the dairymaid, supposing herself to have made a brilliant match only to discover that she was even more impoverished than before," Margaret observed.

James regarded her quizzically. "Indeed it must. It should serve as a lesson to anyone who thinks of marriage as nothing more than an opportunity for material gain."

"I hope they were happy," Amanda said with a sigh. "They sacrificed so much for each other."

While the three Darringtons speculated on the probable fate of Lord Robert and his bride, James examined the other works of art adorning the walls. Except for an enormous landscape over the sofa, these were portraits of various members of the Montford family, as evidenced by the dark coloring and prominent nose. The full significance of this latter feature, however, did not dawn on him until he found himself confronting a silhouette from the previous century. Unlike Miss Amanda's painted handiwork, this one was cut from white vellum and mounted on black paper. But aside from the artist's choice of medium and the long periwigged hair of the subject, it was a near twin of the one tacked onto the wall of his own bedroom. As he stared at the long, slightly concave nose, his hand crept upward to trace the line of the protuberant proboscis that had once been the bane of his school days. A loud roaring filled his ears, and he squeezed his eyes shut against the onslaught of images that assailed his brain. A hundred, a thousand memories came rushing at once into his consciousness: a redhaired schoolboy laughingly calling him Weathervane; a highly unflattering caricature drawn by a recalcitrant young Latin scholar; a bespectacled London solicitor saying, "It is my duty and privilege to inform you . . . ."

His legs suddenly balked at supporting him, and James reached out a shaking hand and grasped the back of the nearest chair. If this were true—and no one comparing the framed silhouette to his own profile could doubt it—then he could have told Mrs. Collins what happened to Lord Robert and his bride. Indeed, he had a duty to do so.

"Mr. Fanshawe?"

Margaret Darrington's voice seemed to be calling him from a very great distance. Focusing his eyes with an effort, he found her regarding him with an expression of concern and bewilderment.

"Mr. Fanshawe, are you all right?"

"Quite—quite all right," James assured her with perhaps less than perfect truth. "It—it is very warm in here, is it not? If you will excuse me, I should like to step outside for a breath of fresh air. I—I shall rejoin you directly."

Having delivered himself of this disjointed speech, he made his escape as if the Furies were at his heels, bumping into a small side table in his haste and almost oversetting a china shepherdess. He set the rocking figure to rights with a vague apology to no one in particular, and reached the safety of the Hall without further mishap.

Here he was faced with a decision. If he truly wanted

fresh air, he could either retrace his steps to the kitchen through which he had come, or he could try and see if the massive oak door opening onto the front portico was unlocked. But even as he weighed these two possibilities, a third and even more tantalizing option presented itself. For directly opposite that front door, the broad staircase stretched upward to the private family rooms above.

Before he was even aware of having made a decision, his hand was on the carved banister, and his foot on the first riser. He chose his steps with care, taking pains to make no noise which might alert the housekeeper even as he acknowledged his own foolishness in skulking like a thief through a house which, if a certain London solicitor was to be believed, now belonged to him.

He reached the top of the stairs, and found a thickly carpeted corridor stretching off to the left and right. After a moment's hesitation, he turned to the left. Here were the rooms where generations of his family had lived out their lives: a music room with a pianoforte positioned before the window and a harp standing in the corner; a library with half a dozen marble busts standing guard over shelf after shelf of calf-bound volumes. Emboldened to explore further, he mounted a less imposing staircase to the next floor. This was the most intimate part of the house, for the rooms lining the corridor on each side were bedchambers, some decorated in delicate pastels, others paneled with wood polished with beeswax until it shone. At last, all that remained was a pair of double doors at the end of the corridor. James pushed them open, and blinked in amazement.

"Good God!"

This bedchamber was much larger than the others, and far more luxuriously decorated. Emerald green silk covered the walls while sumptuous velvet of an identical shade adorned the windows, the lavish folds held back by plump gilt cherubs. Over James's head, more cherubs cavorted across the plastered ceiling. At one end of the room stood a raised dais containing an extravagantly curtained four-poster bed so large that a family of four might comfortably sleep there.

This was unquestionably the duke's own bedchamber. A collection of exotic knick-knacks testified to the travels of some now-departed holder of the title: Carrara marble from Italy, jade from the Orient, gleaming mahogany from Abyssinia. It occurred to James that the dreams of travel he had recently confided to Miss Darrington could now be realized. He took a step forward to examine the collection more closely, and the movement drew his attention to his own image reflected in a large mirror of elaborate rococo design. The contrast could not have been more marked. His worn, sober-hued coat and oft-darned stockings appeared ludicrous amid such splendor. Had the room's previous occupants (particularly the specimen captured on canvas downstairs) not already abandoned it for a place in the family vault, the shock of seeing him, the hope and future of the house of Weatherly, must surely have been sufficient to kill them.

The hope and future of the house of Weatherly . . .

He turned away from the mirror to look once more at the enormous bed. If he was indeed the tenth duke of Montford—and Mr. Mayhew, the London solicitor, seemed quite certain that he was—then he had a responsibility to marry and sire the future eleventh duke of Montford without delay. And this obligation raised yet another hitherto undreamt-of possibility.

He could marry Amanda Darrington.

CHAPTER 8

James's head was still spinning when he rejoined the party downstairs, but he dared not linger in the ducal bedchamber lest someone come searching for him. He found them just settling down to partake of tea and cakes in the housekeeper's room belowstairs, the redoubtable Mrs. Collins having apparently won her point after all.

"Ah, Mr. Fanshawe, there you are," said Margaret, regarding him with a puzzled expression. "We had almost given you up for lost."

Incapable of framing a coherent reply, James merely tossed back the steaming cup of Darjeeling proffered by Mrs. Collins, and wished it were something stronger. Somehow he contrived to choke down a seed cake, striving all the while to behave normally—although what constituted normal behavior for a man who had just remembered inheriting a dukedom, he could not begin to guess.

After what seemed an eternity, the last cake was finally eaten and the last empty teacup set aside. The Darrington sisters thanked Mrs. Collins very prettily for her time, and the foursome began the trek back to Darrington House. As they crested the hill from which vantage point the priory ruins could be seen, James was reminded of the robed figure he had encountered there. Was it possible that he had seen Miss Darrington's ghostly monk? Nonsense, he chided himself. Such things did not happen in real life. Still, the apparition was said to appear only to the heir. The idea that someone—even a specter—had recognized him as such was sufficient to embolden James to put his changed circumstances to the test. As they neared the stile, he took Amanda's arm and assisted her over.

He was rewarded by a shy smile. "Thank you, Mr. Fanshawe." Amanda peeped up at him beneath the wide brim of her gypsy hat. "How very good you are."

James, thinking of the ducal bed, flushed scarlet. "The— the pleasure is all mine, Miss Amanda, I assure you. That is—" he amended hastily, "any way I may be of service to you—"

"Ahem!"

Rescue came from a most unlikely source. Miss Darrington had already navigated the stile under her own steam, and now awaited the pair with displeasure writ large upon her countenance. James realized that he still clasped Miss Amanda's elbow, and released it with some reluctance. For the remainder of the walk, he contented himself with admiring Miss Amanda—his future bride—from a respectful distance. He tried to picture the pair of them joining hands in church, and failed utterly. It was vaguely unsettling to think of her in such terms; she seemed a charming stranger, but nothing more. Far more vivid in his imagination was the highly gratifying scene in which he formally asked the elder Miss Darrington for her sister's hand, and presented that mercenary miss with a proposed marriage settlement that would make her head spin. Would she fall on his neck (an interesting prospect in itself), or would she find it galling to be beholden to the self-same fellow she had once coolly informed of his own ineligibility?

"You have been strangely quiet, Mr. Fanshawe," observed Margaret as they stepped onto the front portico. "I hope our excursion has not proved too much for you."

"No, indeed, I found it—most educational. Still, I

should welcome the chance to rest quietly in my room." He held the front door open for her, and touched her sleeve when she would have passed through it. "First, however, I wonder if I might have a word with you—"

"Margaret, my love, I'm so glad you are here!" cried Aunt Hattie, bursting into the hall with much wringing of hands and twisting of apron. "The collier's boy is here. He was lying in wait for me when I returned from Lady Palmer's. He wants paying, you know, and won't go away without it!"

"Oh, dear! Thank you, Aunt Hattie, I shall settle the matter at once. Mr. Fanshawe, it appears our discussion must wait. If you will excuse me, I shall be with you directly."

She cast her bonnet and gloves onto a nearby chair and strode from the room. James, fully confident of her ability to make short shrift of an insolent village lad, followed as far as the kitchen door and froze on the threshold at the discovery that he had much mistaken the matter. The collier's "boy" was no stripling, but a beefy young man well into his third decade of life. He sprawled in a chair before the fire, taking frequent pulls from the tankard of cider with which Aunt Hattie had attempted to placate him.

"Yes, Ned?" Margaret asked in a voice that brooked no nonsense. "What do you want?"

He looked her up and down insolently, then wiped his mouth on his sleeve and heaved himself to his feet. He took three slow steps in her direction, stopping just a bit closer to her than courtesy allowed. "I want paying. Pa says you're three weeks late already."

Margaret would not demean herself by attempting to deny it. "Yes, I spoke to your father about that a fortnight ago. He agreed to accept payment, with appropriate interest, after the next quarter day."

"I s'pose when you're a fine lady in a big house, you thinks you can pay whenever you please," Ned sneered. "I'll wager you're not so easy-like when it's your tenants what owes *you* money."

Margaret stiffened, but before she could deliver a suitably crushing rejoinder, she felt a movement at her shoulder.

"You will apologize to the lady at once," commanded a voice so haughty and cold she hardly recognized it as the tutor's.

"I meant no offense, I'm sure," mumbled Ned, dropping his gaze. "All I want is what's rightfully mine."

"And so you shall have it," declared James, withdrawing a knitted coin purse from the breast pocket of his coat. "Tell me, how much does Miss Darrington owe?"

Margaret made a faint noise of protest, but James, emptying most of the contents of his coin purse into Ned's large and grimy hand, took no notice.

"Take it and leave this house at once," he ordered the collier's son. "You may assure your father that, since Miss Darrington is such a poor credit risk, she will do your family a singular service and, in future, purchase her coal elsewhere."

"I'm sure I never meant—" Ned began, but something in the tutor's expression made him think better of whatever he was about to say. With much bowing and scraping, and many assurances that there were no hard feelings, he took himself off.

James followed him as far as the door, closed it firmly behind him, and turned back into the kitchen to find Margaret staring at him in disbelieving wonder.

"Miss Darrington?"

"Mr. Fanshawe!" Margaret found her voice, only to lose it again. "You—You—How did you *do* that?"

He grinned sheepishly. "It's not so very difficult, really. One cannot hope to pound Latin into the heads of unwilling schoolboys without developing a certain air of authority."

"Yes, I daresay, but—you should not have paid him, and out of your own wages, at that. Really, Mr. Fanshawe, you should not have done so."

"I beg your pardon if I have overstepped, but it appeared to me to be the only way to be rid of the fellow. I speak from experience; I confess to having owed my share of delinquent bills."

"But what, pray, are you to live on?"

"You may repay me next quarter day with—what was it?—appropriate interest. Until then, my needs are modest, and from what I have seen, the shops of Montford offer little to tempt a man to extravagance. I assure you, Miss Darrington, I shall contrive."

Although this last was accompanied by a show of dimples, Margaret had the distinct impression that argument would be futile and probably undignified as well. After extracting a promise that he would come to her at once if he should unexpectedly find himself in need of funds (although precisely what she might do in this eventuality she was not quite certain), she allowed the issue to drop, and suggested that they rejoin the others before Aunt Hattie shredded her apron to ribbons. Halfway up the stairs, however, another aspect of the matter occurred to her. She turned back to address the tutor, and found herself nose-to-nose with him.

"Oh, Mr. Fanshawe," she began, acutely aware of his unusual height and their unexpectedly close proximity. "I

106

should not wish to appear ungrateful for your efforts on my behalf—in fact, nothing could be further from the truth!—but purely for your own information, I feel I must inform you—"

"Yes, Miss Darrington?" he prompted when her voice faltered.

"You should be aware that there is no one else in Montford from whom one may purchase coal."

"Oh," said James, nonplussed.

"A minor flaw in an otherwise brilliant performance," she assured him.

He grinned down at her. "Never fear, Miss Darrington. I shall chop wood for the fires myself before I would allow you to be bullied by such as Ned."

Upon hearing this declaration, Margaret became aware of a faint fluttering sensation somewhere deep inside. Her fears, however (and fears there certainly were, along with some other, less readily identifiable emotion) were not for anything Ned Collier might choose to do. Instead, she feared anew for her sister's sake. In the years since her father's death, Margaret had forgotten—or perhaps she had never fully known—how very pleasant it was to have a man about the house upon whom one could depend. She had been aware from the time she had encountered him bloody and beaten upon the road that Mr. Fanshawe possessed a certain self-deprecating charm; as his bruises had healed, it had been further impressed upon her that he was also the possessor of a countenance which, if not precisely handsome in the classical sense, was undeniably pleasing to look upon. Until he had routed the boorish Ned, however, it had not occurred to her that the tutor she had engaged for her brother embodied, in every particular but that of economics, all any woman might wish for in a husband. Surely it would require more strength of character than her sister possessed to resist such a paragon.

"I—I believe you wanted to speak with me, Mr. Fanshawe?" she stammered, unaccountably tongue-tied.

He shook his head. "I seem to have—forgotten—what I intended to say."

"I daresay Ned drove it from your mind."

He did not deny this suggestion, although nothing could have been further from the truth. In fact, it was precisely because of Ned that he could not say what he had intended. Miss Darrington was undoubtedly embarrassed at having her straitened circumstances called to his attention; he would not add to her humiliation by informing her that she now stood indebted to the duke of Montford. No, his confession would have to wait until another day.

Alas, the days that followed offered no better opportunity for confession. All of the morning and much of the afternoon were taken up with Philip's lessons, which, duke or no, James had been engaged to teach. It was true that he dined with the family in the evening, but making such an announcement at the dinner table hardly seemed appropriate. He might, of course, have revealed himself to Miss Amanda while at the same time laying his coronet, figuratively speaking, at her feet. But while this prospect held a certain romantic appeal, James could not feel entirely comfortable with it. No, it was Miss Margaret Darrington who had engaged his services, and it was to her that he must make his confession.

All too quickly, the week was ended and a new one begun, and still James had not revealed his true identity. On Sunday morning, dressed in his best coat and breeches, he sat beside the Darringtons at church and felt the worst sort of hypocrite when the vicar read from the pulpit St. Paul's exhortation to speak the truth in love. In the time-honored tradition of the unrepentant sinner, James argued with his conscience that his own case was different; once he was assured of her love, he reasoned, the truth would take care of itself. In this, however, he knew himself to be doing Amanda less than justice. Although he could not yet claim an intimate acquaintance with his chosen bride, he had seen enough of that young lady to know that if her heart were not engaged, the duke of Montford's suit would stand no greater chance of success than plain Mr. Fanshawe's. No, it was her sister who must be persuaded, and Miss Darrington had given every indication that she would welcome such an exalted match for her sister—indeed, she seemed to expect nothing less. Why, then, was he so reluctant to bring about a conclusion so very satisfactory for all concerned?

James could only be thankful when the youthful vicar (distracted, no doubt, by the sight of Amanda's limpid gaze fixed attentively upon him) wandered from a topic that had become uncomfortably personal. Still, there was no respite for James's conscience, for to his immediate right loomed the elaborately carved Montford family pew, accusing him with its very emptiness.

At last, the vicar wound to a conclusion, the benediction was said, and the parishioners were free to go. But the sermon, however rambling, had done its work: as the Darrington party bade the clergyman farewell at the door and stepped out of the church and into the sunshine, James fell into step beside Margaret and touched her sleeve.

"Miss Darrington, if I might—"

"Ah, Miss Darrington!"

He was interrupted by a tall, angular woman of about fifty years, bearing down upon them with a determined air.

A nattily dressed young man followed in her wake, along with an older gentleman whom James recognized as the magistrate who had interviewed him shortly after his arrival.

"Allow me to present my husband's nephew, who has been positively agog to meet you all," the lady continued. "Mr. Peregrine Palmer, pray make your bow to Mrs. Blaylock, Miss Darrington, Miss Amanda Darrington, Philip Darrington, and Mr.—?" she paused, realizing that she had never met the soberly dressed young man accompanying the family.

Margaret stepped into the breach. "Fanshawe," she put in. "Philip's tutor. Mr. Fanshawe, may I present Lady Palmer, and I am sure you remember Sir Humphrey."

James said all that was proper to the squire and his wife, then turned to the younger man, who regarded him with incredulity writ large upon his countenance.

"*Weathervane?*" exclaimed Mr. Peregrine Palmer, "Good God! What the devil are you—?"

"Yes, it is I, James *Fanshawe*, at your service," James put in quickly, giving his childhood friend a quelling look. "It's good to see you again, Perry. How long has it been?"

"Five years at the least reckoning. So, what have you been doing with yourself lately?" Peregrine asked, the piercing look he gave James giving the lie to his offhand manner.

"I have been engaged as tutor to Philip Darrington."

"The devil you have! I say, are you aware that the whole of London—"

"I fear I don't get up to London very often," James interrupted quickly. "You, on the other hand, have become the complete Town beau! What, pray, do you call that neckcloth?"

"This old thing? Merely the Pastorale—all very well for

the country, you know, but Torrington would laugh himself silly if I were to wear it into White's."

"Torrington? You must tell me—but I fear we shall bore the ladies. There is nothing more tiresome than to be obliged to listen to others reminisce about a set of persons one has never heard of! Do say you will dine with me at the Pig and Whistle on my next half-day, and we may talk about old times to our hearts' content."

Peregrine's smile held such demonic delight that James knew his old friend was not deceived. "Oh, I should like that of all things," Peregrine assured him. "I am bursting to hear all about new times, too!"

Having thoroughly discomposed one member of the party, Peregrine turned his attention to another. "We meet again, fair Ceres," he said, bowing to Amanda.

Amanda curtsied, coloring beneath her best bonnet. "If I had known what an honor was to be mine, sir, I should have pleaded a headache and stayed home."

"Too cruel!" protested Peregrine. "When I have waited every day at the foot bridge, hoping for a glimpse of you—"

"You have not! Why, only yesterday I—" realizing too late her indiscretion, she clapped a small gloved hand over her mouth.

Peregrine crowed with laughter. "Confess, Ceres! You looked for me!"

"I did not!" Amanda protested, painfully aware of the futility of a line of argument which, besides being patently untrue, sounded both childish and undignified.

"I am sorry to have disappointed you, but I have been laid up with an illness, and am only recently arisen from my bed of pain."

"What a pity that your sufferings seem to have affected your wits," retorted Amanda. Uncomfortably aware of

111

coming off the worse in the encounter, she elected to cut her losses by very pointedly turning her back on him and listening with every appearance of rapt attention to Lady Palmer.

"As Peregrine will someday be stepping into my husband's shoes, it seems only fitting that he make the acquaintance of the local families," that redoubtable lady informed Margaret and Aunt Hattie. "I am planning a party to introduce him to the neighborhood gentry. Nothing very grand, only dinner and cards, and I daresay a little dancing for the young people. Do say you will come!"

Aunt Hattie, always a little intimidated by the forceful Lady Palmer, was all eager obeisance. "It sounds most delightful—"

"Dancing!" cried Amanda, eyes aglow. "Will there be waltzing?"

"To be sure, there must be waltzing, or my nephew will think us all sadly rustic."

Amanda clapped her hands in glee, oblivious to her sister's attempts to frown her down.

"You are too gracious, Lady Palmer, but I fear we must decline," Margaret interrupted. "Amanda is not yet out, you know."

Lady Palmer bent an appraising look upon Amanda. "Ah, yes! But this circumstance is shortly to be rectified, is it not?"

Margaret nodded. "We hope to go to London in the spring for her presentation."

"There you have it, then!" pronounced Lady Palmer in a voice that brooked no argument. "I have always felt it did young girls a great deal of good to get their feet wet, so to speak, at smaller functions before thrusting them all unprepared into a London ballroom. Depend upon it, my party will be just the sort of function Amanda needs to develop poise and confidence in her ability to conduct herself in social situations."

It might have been supposed that such a program of self-improvement might hold no attraction for a young lady, but Amanda's eyes shone with enthusiasm as she beseeched her sister.

"Oh, do say we may go, Margaret!"

"Do let's," seconded Aunt Hattie. "As I recall, the Palmer girls all made very eligible matches during their Seasons, so Lady Palmer must certainly know whereof she speaks."

No argument could be more effective in changing Margaret's mind. She threw up her hands, conceding defeat, and turned back to Lady Palmer with a smile. "You see how I am beset, my lady. We shall be delighted to attend."

"Wonderful! And of course you, Mr. Fanshawe, are also included in the invitation, as an old friend of Peregrine's."

"Lord, yes," agreed Peregrine, grinning wickedly at James. "Like Miss Amanda, you must learn how to conduct yourself in social situations. One never knows when one might find oneself, oh, addressing Parliament, for instance, or making one's bow to the Regent!"

It was a very merry group that made its way back to Darrington House. Aunt Hattie and Amanda expounded upon the need for new dresses, and speculated as to the fabrics and trims available at the local dressmaker, while Margaret bethought herself of several gowns remaining from her own long-ago Season which might be cut down and retrimmed. Philip, still too young to attend such a gathering, was only too happy to eschew an entertainment that would require him to do the pretty for the local girls.

James, however, found himself unable to enter into the

general enthusiasm. The truth, he knew, must be told. If he had gone to church that morning to beseech Providence for a sign, the answer could not have been any plainer. For with the appearance of Peregrine Palmer on the scene, everything changed. Peregrine was the best of good fellows, but he had always been a sad rattle, and James could not be sure of his discretion. Much as James disliked having his hand forced, he no longer had the luxury of choosing the most opportune moment.

He did, however, insist upon his right to break the news to Miss Darrington in private. With this end in view, he waited until that night, after Aunt Hattie folded away her needlework and the younger members of the family had departed for their separate bedchambers, to make his confession. He lingered in the privacy of his own bedchamber, pacing the floor while wording and rewording his speech in his head, until the household settled down for the night.

At last reasonably certain of an uninterrupted word with his employer, he abandoned the sanctity of his own room and crept downstairs, candle in hand, to the study, where he hoped to find Miss Darrington; although he had not taken part in the discussion on new gowns, he had been sufficiently aware of it to suspect that she might even now be scouring the household accounts for the wherewithal to clothe the beauteous Miss Amanda in finery suitable for that young lady's rural debut.

His theory proved accurate. Margaret sat alone in the darkened study, poring over an open ledger. A single candle illuminated the pages, casting a golden circle of light that turned her light-brown hair to burnished copper. James wondered why the local lads had never noticed that she was, in her own more subtle way, quite as lovely as her sister.

Pushing aside the irrelevant thought, he raised his hand to rap lightly on the frame of the open door. An abrupt movement on her part, however, stayed his fingers scant inches from the doorframe. As he watched, she pulled a sheet of paper across the desk and began to make a series of rapid calculations, scowling at the results before trying again. James, having had his share of experience at this same task, had no difficulty in recognizing a desperate yet futile attempt to coerce numbers into performing functions of which they were wholly incapable. Slowly, so as not to attract her attention, he lowered his arm back down to his side. As he debated the most tactful way to make his presence known, she laid aside her pen and, propping her elbows on the desk, dropped her head into her hands in a gesture replete with quiet despair.

James, feeling like a voyeur, stepped back into the shadows, and found himself shaking with an unaccountable anger. Why should she be put to such shifts, all so that her sister might not be obliged to wear a made-over gown? Why, for that matter, should she be so determined to sell Amanda to the highest bidder that she gave no thought to finding a husband of her own? Granted, her Season might not have been an unmitigated success, but at four-and-twenty, she was hardly on the shelf. The stubborn wench might still marry someone like—like—

Like me. The answer hit him with all the force of a blow. As with Saul on the Damascus road, the scales fell from his eyes, and he knew why he had been so reluctant to press his suit, now that he had the wherewithal to do so. Ever since he had first taken up residence in the Darrington household, it had been Margaret Darrington, not her sister, whose company he consistently sought out. Amanda's chief attraction—aside from the obvious—lay in the fact that through marriage to her, he might have the satisfaction of lightening her sister's load, thus earning Miss Darrington's gratitude, respect, and admiration. Particularly admiration. Now, for the first time, he allowed himself to imagine what it would be like to be married, not to Miss Amanda, but to her sister. The prospect was surprisingly pleasant and somehow *right*, even—perhaps especially—down to the sharing of the great ducal bed upstairs at Montford Park.

But this would not be his first proposal of marriage. There had been another, and although his heart had obviously recovered, his pride had not. He had no more desire to be accepted for wealth by Margaret Darrington than by the faraway belle of Fairford. True, he had an advantage this time that he had not before. He might remove himself to the big Palladian house on the hill, trick himself out in fine clothes, and make her an offer in form, but he would always wonder whether she was marrying *him*—James Weatherly—or the long wondered-about duke of Montford.

Of course, there was another option. One had only to look at the armies of ancient Greece and Troy to see that a stealth campaign might succeed where a frontal assault would fail. He could stay where he was, as Philip's tutor, and woo her in earnest. Although she had left him in no doubt as to her opinion of his eligibility as a husband for her sister, he flattered himself that she did not find him utterly repulsive.

Shielding his candle with his cupped hand, he backed away from the study and crept back up the stairs to his room. The matter was settled. Tomorrow he would begin to lay siege to his love's rather avaricious affections, but when at last he made his proposal, it would be as Mr. James Fanshawe, former curate and sometime Latin tutor.

CHAPTER 9

The following day seemed particularly designed to contrast with the merriment of the one before. The sky, so blue and dotted with puffy white clouds a scant twenty-four hours earlier, was now gray and overcast, the clouds heavy with incipient rain. A further pall descended at breakfast, where Margaret imparted the news to her sister and aunt that there would be no new gowns for the Palmers' entertainment. Amanda bore the disappointment nobly, but although she voiced no complaint, her downcast eyes and trembling lower lip spoke volumes.

An awkward silence greeted this pronouncement, and Margaret, finding herself the object of her aunt's silent reproaches and the tutor's searching gaze, became uncomfortably aware of having been cast as the villain of the piece. Only Philip, tucking into his breakfast with the enthusiasm of the adolescent male, seemed oblivious to the silent drama being enacted at the breakfast table.

"It is only a country party, after all," she reminded her sister somewhat defensively, as if refuting an unspoken accusation. "Only wait until your presentation in the spring, dearest, and you shall have all the new gowns your heart can desire."

Amanda's smile was brave, if somewhat shaky. "Oh yes, I am sure I will. It is not as if I particularly wanted to impress anyone, anyway."

At that moment, the skies opened and the rains fell in earnest. When Amanda Darrington grieved, reflected Margaret bitterly, all Nature mourned.

"Still," Margaret added on a brighter note, "there is no reason why we cannot cut down one of my own presentation gowns for you. As I recall, there is a white muslin that should look lovely on you."

"And what will you wear, Margaret dear?" asked Aunt Hattie.

"I have not given the matter much thought," she answered with perhaps less than perfect truth. "I daresay my blue satin will serve the purpose very well."

"That old thing?" cried Aunt Hattie, aghast. "Why, it is ages old!"

"Nonsense! Three years at the very most. Surely styles have not changed so very much in three years."

"I could not feel right wearing something new—even if it was only remade—while you wore an old gown," protested Amanda.

"And quite right, too," nodded Aunt Hattie. "Margaret, if anyone is to wear one of your presentation gowns, it should be you."

"And a fine figure I should look, too, dressing like a debutante at my age! 'Mutton dressed as lamb,' Lady Palmer would say, and she would be quite right."

Another man intent upon courtship might have seized the opportunity to offer flowery compliments to his inamorata's youth and beauty, but James, seated at the opposite end of the table, kept his own counsel. It was not that he had nothing to say in opposition to Margaret's unflattering assessment of her own charms—quite the contrary. But he knew his opinionated love well enough to realize that any such attempt on his part would be disbelieved at best, and very likely laughed to scorn as well. He would hold his tongue until he won the right to speak what was in his heart, and when the time came he would not air his opinions at the breakfast table; his thoughts on the subject were for her ears alone. In the meantime, he left to Aunt Hattie and Amanda the task of chiding Margaret, and bore his pupil upstairs to the schoolroom where Homer awaited.

Deprived of male company, the ladies gave themselves over to the delights of debating ribbons and laces, and eventually abandoned the breakfast table in favor of the humbler confines of the attic, where the trunks containing Margaret's finery were stored.

As her sister and aunt removed the protective tissue from each gown, exclaiming over the prospects for restoring it to the current fashion, Margaret could not suppress a pang of regret for the girl who had once put on these gowns with such eagerness. So many youthful hopes and dreams, and what had become of them? She had not met the man she could love, much less marry, and it seemed highly unlikely now that she ever would. What would become of her? Would she end her days like Aunt Hattie, a maiden aunt to Amanda or Philip's children? In recent years she had begun to accept that this would most probably be her lot, and it had seemed no great tragedy; Aunt Hattie, after all, was held in great affection by her nieces and nephew. But then, Aunt Hattie was no spinster; she was a widow who had once loved and been loved in return, however briefly. Suddenly life as a maiden aunt no longer seemed desirable, although Margaret could not have said with certainty when, or why, her views on the matter had changed.

You are becoming maudlin, she chided herself. She had not slept well the previous night, and this was the result. Determined to be cheerful, she wedged herself between her sister and aunt and, withdrawing a pale primrose frock from the trunk, began to relate a long and rather involved anec-

119

dote about the long-ago ball to which she had worn it.

Amanda's enthusiasm, however, soon proved to be contagious, and when Aunt Hattie unearthed an all-but-forgotten creation of lilac lace over a white satin slip (which, ironically, had been judged too sophisticated for a young girl just emancipated from the schoolroom), it was unanimously determined Margaret would be foolish to appear at Lady Palmer's party in anything else.

Margaret was not so sunk in the dismals that she could not appreciate the irony of that same schoolgirl, still unmarried, fretting over whether that too-sophisticated gown was now too youthful. By the time the family reconvened that afternoon for tea, she was looking forward to the Palmer entertainment with something approaching enthusiasm, and was able to join the others in describing to James the various people he might expect to meet.

"Only beware the Widow Thornton," cautioned Aunt Hattie, gesturing ominously with a butter knife. "Don't let that fragile air deceive you. The woman is a harpy, plain and simple."

"Why, Aunt!" cried Amanda, "how can you say so? She gave me my first lessons on the pianoforte, and I have often heard the vicar say the Ladies' Altar Guild would be lost without her."

Aunt Hattie gave a most unladylike snort. "She may fool them all, but she cannot fool me! She once won ten shillings from me at whist, and you will never convince me she was not cheating!"

Philip Darrington rolled his eyes toward the ceiling, and this, along with his sisters' sudden preoccupation with the buttering of scones, gave James to understand that this particular grievance was not a new one.

Seeing that the rôle of outraged audience fell to him,

James stepped gamely into the breach. "Such perfidy must not be allowed to go unchallenged," he declared in tones of deepest revulsion. "If you will allow me, Aunt Hattie, I will set up a card table after tea. I feel certain that with a little practice, we may win your ten shillings back."

Philip volunteered to help make up a foursome, and Margaret agreed to make a fourth, if for no other reason than to prevent James from soliciting Amanda for that honor. She was gratified to hear that damsel profess herself more than willing to forego a diversion for which she had no natural aptitude, but any hope that this might indicate an indifference for the tutor was short-lived; she was familiar enough with Amanda's indifferent play to know that no young lady in the throes of a violent *tendre* would want the object of her affections to see her displayed to such disadvantage.

As soon as the tea cart was removed, a once-fine card table of inlaid rosewood took its place, and the card players settled down to the business of shuffling, cutting, and dealing.

"What about stakes?" fretted Aunt Hattie. "Shall we play for penny points?"

"Pennies?" echoed James. "Nothing so paltry! I shall stake my curricle and pair against Miss Darrington's pearls."

"Done," replied Margaret, her fine eyes sparkling in anticipation.

Philip looked bewildered. "But you don't have a curricle and pair!"

James smiled at Margaret. "Then I shan't suffer overmuch if Miss Darrington deprives me of it."

"Oh, I see!" cried Philip. "In that case, I shall stake my dueling pistols against Aunt Hattie's diamond brooch."

"Oh, but I could not!" exclaimed Aunt Hattie, aghast. "It belonged to my dear mother, you know."

Margaret patted her hand. "It's quite all right, my dear. It is only make-believe."

Aunt Hattie's brow cleared immediately. "Oh! In that case, Philip, I must tell you that while I have no use for dueling pistols, I have always admired that pretty little gray mare of yours."

As the mare in question existed only in Aunt Hattie's imagination, Philip did not hesitate to offer it as a stake. A very jolly hour followed, at the end of which Aunt Hattie and James were the proud possessors of both Margaret's pearls and Philip's mare, along with a castle in Spain, a hunting-box in Leicestershire, and a seaside cottage in Brighton.

"I only hope that Widow Thornton has a very large supply of coins," Aunt Hattie said, rubbing her hands together in anticipatory glee, "for I intend to reclaim my ten shillings."

"Don't forget to fleece her for a few more while you are about it," recommended James. "Interest, you know."

Aunt Hattie beamed at her cohort. "I am sure I cannot help but do so, for no one else will have half so able a partner."

"I hate to be the one to dash your hopes, Aunt, but I fear you will have to find another partner," said Margaret, gathering up the playing cards. "Mr. Fanshawe will be occupied elsewhere."

"I will?" This was clearly news to James.

"Yes, indeed! You heard Lady Palmer; there will be dancing. All the young ladies will think themselves very ill-used if you do not dance with them at least once."

"I had no idea I was so desirable a partner," confessed

James, regarding her with a quizzical smile. "In fact, I have recently been given to understand just the opposite."

Margaret colored, but refused to take the bait. "Surely you must have noticed that Montford is sadly lacking in young men. Lady Palmer—and everyone else, for that matter—will expect you to do your duty." She regarded him sharply as a new and not wholly unwelcome thought occurred. "You do dance, Mr. Fanshawe?"

His smile broadened into a grin, leaving Margaret with the uncomfortable feeling that he could read her mind. "Indeed I do, Miss Darrington. And let me say that I will do my utmost to see that Miss Amanda does not languish against the wall."

Amanda, who had been following the conversation only half-heartedly, looked up at the mention of her name. "Oh, Mr. Fanshawe, do you waltz? Can you teach me?"

"You forget that Mr. Fanshawe has been obliged to earn his bread," Margaret reminded her. "I doubt he has had the luxury of cavorting about the ballroom in three-quarter time."

James gave an apologetic little cough. "Er, as a matter of fact, I do waltz a bit," he confessed. Seeing the look on Margaret's face, he was driven by some demon of vanity to add, "I am generally accounted to be quite good at it."

Margaret's smile was somewhat stiff. "I stand corrected. No doubt you were once the beau of Almack's."

He grinned back at her, clearly enjoying her chagrin. "Hardly. But in my previous situation, I was acquainted with a lady very much like Miss Amanda. She was young and very lovely, and she loved to dance above all things. It was common knowledge that any gentleman desirous of winning her favor—and there were many—must first master the waltz."

"I scent a romance!" cried Aunt Hattie with one of those rare flashes of insight that occasionally disconcerted her young relatives. "Tell us, Mr. Fanshawe, were you successful?"

"In becoming the lady's favorite partner for the waltz, perhaps, but nothing more."

"Then you must be very proficient indeed," exclaimed Amanda. "Pray, would you teach me to waltz? Then Meg will not be obliged to go to the expense of hiring a dancing master in London," she added, effectively silencing her sister's protests.

"I should be honored, Miss Amanda."

Philip, taking his cue, returned the card table to its usual corner. Aunt Hattie eagerly offered her services as musician, and after a brief search for a suitable piece, selected a German folk dance and settled herself at the pianoforte. To Margaret's surprise, however, it was not Amanda but herself to whom the tutor held out his hand.

"Shall we perform a demonstration first?"

Margaret, taken aback, shook her head. "I—I fear I cannot oblige you, Mr. Fanshawe. You see, I made my come-out seven years ago, before the waltz was widely performed. I have never learned it myself."

"Worse and worse!" declared James in mock horror. "Miss Amanda, I hope you will pardon me if I give your sister her lesson first. Her advanced age, you know, makes it imperative that we waste no more time. She may not have many good years left."

As Amanda giggled and Philip hooted, James took Margaret by the hand and led her to the middle of the room.

"Now you are mocking me," she chided him.

"Not at all," he assured her, settling his arm about her waist. "I am mocking all the men who have allowed you to go unclaimed for so long."

Margaret was struck with the realization that it had been far too long since she had danced, for they had scarcely begun and already her heart was racing and her breath came in shallow gasps, as if her stays were too tight.

It soon transpired that James had not exaggerated his own proficiency. He possessed the musician's innate sense of rhythm, and although he stood a head taller than his partner, he obligingly shortened his long strides to match her own shorter steps. Even after an extended absence from the dance floor, Margaret found it surprisingly easy to follow his lead—so easy, in fact, that she felt as if she might close her eyes and feel as if she were flying. Nor was she alone in her enjoyment of the exercise; she was vaguely aware of Amanda beaming at them from the sofa, and even Philip, turning pages for Aunt Hattie, appeared impressed. As for Aunt Hattie, her efforts on the pianoforte demanded most of her attention, but when she reached a familiar passage in the music, she glanced up at the dancers and sighed wistfully, "What a handsome couple they make!"

Margaret's right foot was immediately transformed into a second and altogether superfluous—left. She missed a step, caught her toe in the carpet, and pitched forward, falling heavily against James's chest. His arms closed about her at once, but although this gesture was undoubtedly meant to steady her on her feet, it somehow had quite the opposite effect.

"Did I step on your foot?" She looked up to find James gazing down at her in some concern. "If so, I beg your pardon."

"No, no, you dance very well," she assured him breathlessly. She summoned up a shaky smile for reassurance. "But I am sadly out of practice, as you can see."

His brow puckered thoughtfully. "Yes, I can see that. Perhaps we should try again?"

"No, no!" she said hastily, holding up her hands as if to ward him off. "I fear I have had my fill of dancing for one day."

"My turn now!" cried Amanda, all but bouncing up and down in her seat.

So great was Margaret's inner turmoil that she scarcely noticed James leading her sister into the dance. Gradually, however, she became aware of Amanda's laughing face lifted up to his, all flushed cheeks and sparkling eyes, and feared she was fighting a losing battle. If the family's fortunes were to be salvaged, she must dismiss Mr. Fanshawe before he succeeded in attaching Amanda's affections. Unfortunately, his wages were now in arrears, thanks to the machinations of Ned Collier, and she had no way of paying them until next quarter day. Until then, she could only hope that Lady Palmer's party would give Amanda such a thirst for frivolity that marriage to a humble tutor, no matter how pleasant his company, would pale beside the prospect of a Season in London.

CHAPTER 10

On Wednesday, his half-day, James set Philip the task of translating a passage from Cicero, then accompanied the two Misses Darrington to the village of Montford, where he was to dine with Mr. Peregrine Palmer while Margaret and Amanda shopped. He parted from them at the emporium and made his way to the Pig and Whistle, where he found Peregrine lying in wait for him.

"Thank God you're here at last!" exclaimed that impatient young man, abandoning his chair near the window of the taproom. "I was beginning to wonder if you'd been coshed on the head again."

"No, merely leaving instructions for my pupil. Some of us must work for our bread, you know," James added meekly.

Peregrine, undeceived, merely snorted. "Try that one on someone else, your Grace."

"Shh!" James cast a furtive glance about the public room, but the only other occupants were too deeply engrossed in a private debate concerning a rash of chicken thefts to pay any heed to the doings of the local gentry.

"I've bespoken nuncheon for us in the private parlor, where we may talk undisturbed," Peregrine said, steering his friend into this chamber and closing the door behind them. "Now, tell me: are you aware that the whole of England is searching for the missing duke of Montford?"

"Are they indeed? Well, I am sorry for it, but they will have to go on searching for him a bit longer."

"Good God, you must be mad!" exclaimed Peregrine.

James's denial of this accusation was forestalled by the entrance of the landlord, bearing a tray loaded with a steaming pork pie, a wedge of cheese, and two foaming tankards of ale. After arranging these with care upon the table (an exercise which, to Peregrine's mind, took an unconscionably long time), he bowed himself from the room.

"By the bye," said James, seating himself at the table, "I hope you won't mind standing squire, as I'm rather pressed for funds at the moment."

"Not at all," drawled Peregrine. "It is always my pleasure to help out a duke in need."

"I can repay you next quarter day—or possibly earlier, if all goes well."

"If all *what* goes well? What the devil are you about, anyway?"

James cut into the pie and placed a slice on each of two pewter plates. "If I promise to tell you, will you sit down and stop pacing? You're giving me a crick in the neck." Peregrine obeyed, flinging himself unceremoniously onto the chair opposite, and James embarked upon what appeared likely to be a lengthy explanation. "I never set out to deceive, at least not at first. I was serving as curate to Fairford parish when a solicitor arrived from London to inform me of my inheritance. When I came to Montford to claim it, I was set upon by footpads, and left with no memory of who I was or where I had come from."

Whatever he had expected, this explanation was clearly not it. "No! It can't be!"

"If you require proof, I am happy to oblige." James pushed a lock of golden hair from his forehead, revealing the faint discoloration of a bruise that had not yet fully healed.

"Oh, I believe you; in fact, my uncle described the incident to me the very day it occurred. By God, James, if I'd had any notion it was you, I would have—"

"You would no doubt have come charging to my rescue, and ruined everything into the bargain. Oh, yes! It is very wrong of me, I know, but I have discovered I rather like being plain Mr. Fanshawe."

"Poppycock!"

"Quite true, I assure you. Mr. Fanshawe, you see, enjoys certain advantages the poor old duke could only dream of."

"Such as—?"

"Such as the satisfaction of knowing that if and when a certain lady agrees to marry him, it will be for himself and not his title."

"I see." Peregrine's smile was somewhat forced. "She— she is very lovely, is she not?"

"I find her so. And not just in the common way, either."

"I think you do her an injustice, though. Surely she is not the sort to marry where her heart is not engaged."

James gave a short bark of laughter. "How can you say so, when I have it from her own lips that she intends to marry off her sister to a wealthy man? Is it likely that she would turn down such a match for herself?"

"Marry off her—?" Peregrine shook his head as if to clear it. "James, which Miss Darrington is it that you wish to marry?"

"Margaret, the elder." Behind his spectacles, James's blue eyes grew wide with dawning comprehension. "Oh, so your interests lie in Miss Amanda's direction, do they? Well, here's hoping I may soon have cause to call you brother."

Tankards were raised to toast this happy prospect, and then Peregrine, after taking a long pull, spoke. "There you are, then! If you know Miss Darrington wants an advantageous marriage for her sister, she must surely snap up an offer from the duke of Montford."

"Therein lies the problem." James's expression grew wistful, and he gazed unseeing out the window. "It will not be the first proposal of marriage I have ever made. There was another, back in Fairford. She was beautiful and flirtatious, and I flattered myself that she returned my regard. But she, too, had her sights set on a London Season and a brilliant match."

"James, you sly dog! Who was she? Would I know her?"

"If you were in London during the spring, you may have met her, or at least heard of her. Her name was Prescott. Cynthia Prescott."

Peregrine pursed his lips and gave a long, low whistle. "The Peerless Miss Prescott? You did fly high, didn't you?"

James grimaced. "And as Icarus reminds us, those who fly too near the sun inevitably get burned."

"And so now you roam about the countryside disguised as a beggar like a prince from a fairy tale, in search of a woman who may love you for yourself alone," crowed Peregrine. "Lord, how rich! You, of all people, who were always the one to caution the rest of us against the worst of our excesses!"

"Did I?" asked James, appalled by this vision of himself. "Good God, what a prosy bore I must have been!"

"Oh, no! You never bored us, for we never paid you the slightest heed," Peregrine assured him, grinning. "Except, of course, when we came running to you to rescue us from our various scrapes. I must say, though, your sober disposition does make your present predicament all the more extraordinary."

James sketched an ironic little bow. "I am gratified to

know that I am providing such excellent entertainment for you."

"Look here, James." Peregrine leaned forward, his expressive countenance suddenly serious. "I know the heart is its own master, and all that, but feeling as you do, is it wise to fix your hopes on a lady as—well, *ambitious* as Miss Darrington?"

"Oh, but I don't think she is—at least, not for her own sake. But she has been carrying far too heavy a load for far too long, with very little assistance."

"I confess I find it hard to take so sympathetic a view of one who would force sweet, innocent Amanda Darrington into marriage with a rich old man."

"I believe you have a point there," marveled James, much struck. "Although we did debate the eligibility of brutes and half-wits, I do not believe any mention was made of the prospective bridegroom's age."

"Brutes? Half-wits? What the devil—?"

"Never mind," said James, laughing aloud at his friend's bewilderment. "I shall explain it later. But come, Perry! You are worldly enough to know that the Misses Darrington have few other options besides marriage, save for dwindling into poverty-stricken spinsterhood. Would you prefer to see Miss Amanda obliged to hire herself out as a governess?"

Peregrine recalled the cringing, colorless female charged with the thankless task of educating his flighty young sisters, and barely repressed a shudder. "Good God, no!"

"Then perhaps in future you will be less critical of Miss Darrington's decisions."

A hint of steel undergirded James's pleasant tenor voice, and his engaging smile grew decidedly wintry. Peregrine stiffened, ready to take offense, but even as his eyes flashed and his nostrils flared, the absurdity of the situation struck him. He threw back his head and laughed.

"And to think I had trouble picturing you as a duke until this moment! As they say, blood will out. Speaking of which—" He reached into the pocket of his coat and withdrew a sheaf of papers bearing a broken seal of red wax. "I have something that belongs to you."

His memory now fully restored, James recognized Peregrine's burden at once. He unfolded the sheets of crackling vellum and spread them upon the table. "I never thought to see these again! Where did you find them?"

"Beneath a hedge on the Montford road."

"I say, is that my blood? That must have given you a rare turn!"

"I should say it did! I fully expected to discover your lifeless body 'round the next curve."

"And I, for one, am very glad you did not. Still, I think I had best ask you to keep these for me yet a while longer," said James, folding the papers together and pushing them across the table toward his friend. "It would not do for one of the Darringtons to discover them."

"Very well, they shall remain safely hidden until King Cophetua has won his beggar-maid!"

James, having caught sight of the clock over the mantel, let this sally pass with no more response than an appreciative grin. Citing the need to return to Darrington House and check on his pupil's progress, he thanked Peregrine for his discretion, and the two young men parted on excellent terms. Peregrine remained behind long enough to settle the bill—shaking his head at the irony of being obliged to stand squire for a man who could buy him several times over— then tugged gloves of York tan over his well-shaped hands, set a curly-brimmed beaver on his head at a jaunty angle, picked up the sheaf of papers still lying on the table, and departed the premises.

He was hauled up short at the sight of a charming figure in green sprigged muslin emerging from a shop on the other side of the street with a basket over one arm. Without further ado, he hurried across the street to intercept Amanda Darrington.

"Well met, Miss Amanda," he said, sweeping an elaborate bow. "And just in time, too, as you are obviously in need of assistance. Pray allow me to carry your basket."

"It is not at all heavy," she protested. "It contains nothing more burdensome than ribbons and lace."

"On the contrary, I also see a paper of pins, and nothing can be more wearisome than to be obliged to haul pins about the countryside," retorted Peregrine, wresting the basket from her unresisting grasp. "But I gather from the contents of your basket that you are soon to be occupied with your needle. Are you to have a new gown for my aunt's party?"

Amanda, seeing the way he commandeered her basket, recalled that she disliked Mr. Palmer excessively. Still, she saw no need to make him privy to the information that she was not making a new gown but retrimming an old one. Rather than disabuse him of this false assumption, she merely nodded.

Peregrine dropped James's papers into the basket, the better to take Amanda's arm. "Will you save a dance for me? The first waltz, perhaps?"

Amanda's heart beat faster at the thought of whirling about the ballroom in Mr. Palmer's arms, but she was determined to put this presumptuous young man in his place. "You are very kind, Mr. Palmer, but I fear I must decline. It is only fitting that I should reserve the first waltz for Mr.

Fanshawe, since he was kind enough to teach me the steps."

"Your scruples do you credit, Miss Amanda, but I feel I should caution you that Mr. Fanshawe intends to solicit your sister for that honor." He regarded her with limpid brown eyes. "I warn you not from any self-serving motive, of course, but only that you may not find yourself languishing against the wall for lack of a partner."

Amanda's urge to give Mr. Palmer a set-down warred briefly but violently with her desire to attempt the new and slightly scandalous dance that had taken London by storm. The end, however, was never really in doubt. "Very well, Mr. Palmer, the first waltz is yours. I should hate to find myself a wallflower, and Aunt Hattie assures me that it is the height of incivility to decline one gentleman's solicitation to dance only to accept when a better—I mean, *another*—offer comes along."

He grinned appreciatively at this home thrust. "It is a great relief to me to know that you rate my charms higher than those of the wall, at all events. But let us leave off pulling caps! Have you finished your shopping? May I escort you home?"

Amanda had indeed finished her shopping, but she was not at all certain she was ready to have done "pulling caps," as Peregrine had so inelegantly phrased it. In fact, she was not quite sure which she found the most objectionable: the skill with which he had manipulated her into promising him the first waltz, or the eagerness with which she had seized upon the first available excuse for doing so. She suspected that to meet with a rebuff must do Mr. Peregrine Palmer a great deal of good, and she was gratified to be presented with a second chance to render him this humble service.

"Escort me home?" she echoed with no small sense of

satisfaction. "I fear I must decline, sir, for I promised my sister that I would meet her at the apothecary after I had finished at the emporium."

"Very well, then I shall have two lovely ladies to attend, rather than just one."

"By all means, sir, since you are so determined. Although I have no doubt you will look very silly trudging along behind our gig."

"Oh, cruel!" Still retaining his grasp on her elbow, he began to steer her in the direction of the apothecary's shop. "If you will have it, then, the apothecary it is."

"I assure you, your gallantry is misplaced," protested Amanda, grabbing ineffectually for her basket. "I am quite capable of finding the apothecary on my own. It is only a step away."

"Just so. Surely my company for so brief a time cannot be so very objectionable."

"You underestimate yourself, sir."

Peregrine merely grinned, his withers unwrung. "I wonder, Miss Amanda, what I can have done to give you such a disgust of me?"

In fact, Amanda was not entirely sure upon this head herself. It was not as if she had never been the object of masculine admiration before—no, indeed! Every man in Montford had attempted to flirt with her at one time or another, from callow youths who stammered out incoherent compliments to grandfatherly types who chucked her under the chin and called her a pretty piece. But there was something distinctly different about Mr. Peregrine Palmer's attentions, something she was not at all certain she liked. To be sure, he paid her all manner of extravagant compliments, but she could not shake the uncomfortable conviction that he did not mean a single one of them. Indeed, it seemed at times almost as if he were mocking her.

One could hardly make a present of this information to such a discommoding gentleman, however, so in the end she was forced to fall back upon a disdainful sniff and the retort of wronged females since Eve. "If you do not know what you have done, it would clearly be useless of me to try and tell you."

It was enough. Peregrine lapsed into grinning silence for the duration of the short walk to the apothecary, where he exchanged civil greetings with Margaret before handing both ladies into their gig. It was not until after the rutted village streets had given way to the open road that Margaret inquired as to the success of Amanda's mission.

"The ribbons and laces, I mean," she explained, finding her sister apparently wool-gathering. "I trust you were able to find something suitable?"

"Oh, yes indeed," Amanda agreed hastily, with only slightly feigned enthusiasm. "Only wait until you see—"

As she reached into the basket, however, it was not ribbons and laces that met her fingers, but a thick packet of papers bearing a broken seal of red wax. Amanda was generally a very well-behaved girl, but such a temptation was not easy to resist; she, in any case, was not proof against it. She unfolded the crackling sheets and scanned the first page.

Margaret, intent upon keeping her sway-backed hack from wandering off the road to sample the grasses growing along the ditch, spared a quick glance for her curiously silent sister. "What do you have there, Amanda?"

"Nothing!" Amanda dropped the papers back into the basket as if they had burned her, and clenched her fingers tightly in her lap in an effort to control their violent trembling. "That is, only some papers Mr. Palmer mislaid."

"Does it appear to be anything important? Should we turn back, or perhaps stop by Sir Humphrey's—?"

"No, no!" Amanda objected, fully cognizant of the absurdity of her protests. *Not important,* indeed! "That is, it appears to be nothing that will not keep until next Sunday, when I may return them to him at church."

Margaret appeared to accept this answer, for which Amanda was grateful. She did not want to tell her sister—not yet, not until she had some time in which to ponder the implications of her discovery before coming face-to-face with its object. The prospect of such a meeting filled her with dread. For although much of the legal language escaped her, the gist of those papers was clear: the young man she knew as Mr. Peregrine Palmer was, in fact, the duke of Montford. She was not quite certain why he was visiting the Palmers under a false name, nor why the very correct Lady Palmer should support him in this deception, but she supposed the duke of Montford must have at his command methods of persuasion which were denied the mere Miss Amanda Darringtons of this world.

The duke of Montford! Small wonder she had so often suspected him of mocking her. He probably found it vastly amusing that a mere country nobody might suppose even for an instant that his attentions were serious. She derived what satisfaction she could from the knowledge that she had never given him the least encouragement, but since her treatment of him had been uncivil to the point of rudeness, this was but small comfort. The party to which she had looked forward with such eager anticipation now loomed before her as ominously as Judgment Day to the infidel. How would she ever face him? Yet face him she must, for she had promised him—indeed, he had all but demanded!—the first waltz. Nor did the prospect of her imminent removal to London offer respite, for when Mr. Palmer returned to Town (she *would* persist in thinking of him as Mr. Palmer, rather than his Grace!) he would doubtless tell all his friends of her impertinence. Her Season would be over before it had even begun, for surely no gentleman of sense would wish to marry such a rag-mannered creature as she. Her whole family would suffer, and all because she had foolishly allowed her head to be turned by the first London beau to cross her path.

Staring bleakly at the road unwinding before her, she returned only half-hearted monosyllables to Margaret's recitation of the latest village gossip. If only she had not insisted on new trimmings for her sister's old gown! But she had fancied herself too fine a bird to wear secondhand feathers, and now she would pay the price for her vanity. As for precisely why she had thought it so important to have a new gown for the occasion, her bruised heart shied away from too keen an analysis.

Arriving at Darrington House on foot only a few minutes ahead of the ladies' gig, James entered the drawing room just in time to see Aunt Hattie, sitting beside the fire reading a letter by its flickering light, suddenly leap to her feet and clasp the single sheet of vellum to her ample bosom in a manner that could only be described as clandestine.

"Love letters, Aunt Hattie?" he chided teasingly. "Fie on you!"

At any other time she would have laughed and scolded him fondly, but today she flushed as guiltily as if she had been discovered rolling about on the carpet with the butcher's boy. "Oh, Mr.—! Oh, how you startled me!"

His smile faded, replaced with an expression of concern.

"I can see that. I beg your pardon. I hope nothing is amiss?"

"No, no! It is only that—it was an honest mistake," she babbled. "My eyesight is not what it was, you know, and although I see now that it was meant for dear Margaret, I had already started reading by that time, and—well, I could not stop."

Having delivered this disjointed explanation (of what, precisely, James still was not quite certain), she appeared to have run out of words. She held out the letter in surrender, and James, curiosity getting the better of him, took it and scanned the shaky script.

Dear Miss Darrington, it read, *I fear you can have no very high opinion of me after my failure either to meet you at the appointed time and place or to inform you of my change of plans. Please believe that only the direst of circumstances could have compelled me to behave in such a fashion. In fact, only two days before my departure for Montford, I was stricken with a violent attack of influenza, which, my physician informs me, settled upon my lungs. After many days in which it seemed uncertain as to whether I should live or die, I have only recently marshaled sufficient strength to put quill to parchment. I hope your young brother has not fallen too far behind in his studies as a result of my absence. I am assuming you have already engaged another tutor to take my place, but if you still have need of my services, you have only to write, and I shall join you as soon as my physician gives me permission to travel.*

Sincerely,

Peter Fanshawe

He stared at the damning paper in his hands for a long moment, then looked up at Aunt Hattie. She regarded him steadily, but her expression was more wounded than accusing. He cleared his throat, opened his mouth to speak, then shut it and cleared his throat again.

"Useless, I suppose, to suggest that it was somehow delayed in the mail and I, now fully recovered, somehow contrived to pass it on the road?"

She shook her head. "Quite, quite useless."

James sighed. "Yes, I suppose one violent attack of influenza and another by footpads are a bit much for one person to endure. I suppose it will have to be the truth, then, insofar as I am able."

"Usually the best course, I have always found," Aunt Hattie observed, waiting expectantly.

James took a deep breath. "Like yours, mine was an honest mistake, at least at first. I truly was set upon by footpads, and left for dead. When I recovered my senses, I had no memory of who I was, where I was, or what I was doing there. Then Miss Darrington came along, and seemed to have no doubts at all upon that head. You will have noticed that your niece is a decisive young woman."

Aunt Hattie, finding nothing in this appraisal with which to take issue, merely nodded.

"I came to Darrington Place, then, supposing myself to be the person Miss Darrington clearly believed me to be. When at last my memory returned, I realized that to reveal the error would make things a bit awkward for everyone. Then there were—other circumstances—which also made it seem best to maintain the *status quo ante,* at least for a time."

Aunt Hattie plunged a hand into her pocket and withdrew a scrap of lace-trimmed cambric, with which she dabbed at her eyes. "Say no more! I confess, I have sometimes wondered if you and—but I must say no more on that head. Only tell me, if you will: if you are not Peter Fanshawe, then who are you?"

"I am not at liberty to say, at least not yet. I must ask you not to give me away to Miss Darrington, but let me tell her myself, as soon as I may see my way clear." Seeing that she was unconvinced, he hastened to add, "I realize I have given you no reason to trust me—quite the opposite, in fact!—but I assure you I mean no harm toward Miss Darrington, or anyone else in your family. Indeed, I hope that I may one day be in a position to—but such speculations are premature. Will you keep my secret, Aunt Hattie?"

Even as she hesitated, assailed by doubts, the front door opened in the hall below and feminine voices wafted up the staircase. Margaret and Amanda had returned. For an endless moment, James and Aunt Hattie's gazes locked in mutual dismay. Then he smiled uncertainly at her, and she came to a decision. She placed the letter on the fire, and together they watched as the paper curled and blackened, and finally burst into flame.

"Thank you, Aunt Hattie." He took her plump hand and raised it to his lips. "Thank you."

CHAPTER 11

The days leading up to the Palmers' entertainment were to live on in Margaret's memory as some of the happiest of her life. To be sure, they were busy ones, as well; the baking, laundering, and other chores necessary to the running of a household would not wait for even the gayest of parties. But in the evenings, after dinner was over and the family relocated to the drawing room, the Darrington sisters and their aunt set to work refurbishing their finery with needle and thread. On these occasions, James fetched the violin from his room and entertained them with music, accompanied more often than not by Philip's rendering of raucous lyrics of his own invention. In such a manner the nights passed swiftly, until at last the long-awaited event was at hand. Margaret, in all the glory of lilac lace over satin, allowed James to hand her into the family's ancient closed carriage, where she took her place beside Aunt Hattie in the vehicle's forward-facing seat.

She could not quite like the sight of Amanda (in stunning looks tonight, although with a hectic color in her cheeks, which Margaret put down to nervous anticipation) sitting next to the tutor in the rear-facing seat, but as they comprised the junior members of the party—Amanda as the younger daughter of the house, and James as its paid employee—there was little Margaret could do about it. To call attention to the seating arrangement, much less to try and alter it, would only imbue it with an importance it did not (she hoped) deserve.

Once inside Sir Humphrey's door, the Darrington party quickly dispersed. Aunt Hattie bore James off to the card room, where he was obliged to endure several hands of whist before good manners would permit him to surrender his place at the table to another, in this case a widowed lady very nearly Aunt Hattie's own age.

Aunt Hattie, it must be said, was not at all pleased with this turn of events. Not only had she enjoyed a very profitable evening with James as her partner, but she was not at all satisfied with the lady who was to act as his substitute.

"Hsst!" she urged in a sibilant whisper. "Not her, I beg you! You must know that lady is—"

Alas, it was too late. James had already risen from his chair, and was settling her nemesis, Mrs. Thornton, in his place with many expressions of gratitude and hopes for her good fortune.

He reached the ballroom (actually the yellow saloon, denuded of its Axminster carpet and most of its furniture in order to accommodate the dancers) just in time to see Margaret led onto the floor by a portly man of middle age. Deprived of his primary object, he settled instead on her sister, and offered Amanda his arm.

In fact, he very nearly missed both of the Darrington sisters, for when he approached her, Amanda was debating the wisdom of hiding behind the large potted palm that filled one corner of the room. One might have supposed her to be having a fine time at her first ball, as she had stood up for every dance, and even had to turn down prospective partners on more than one occasion. But she knew it could not be long before Peregrine was released from his duties as guest of honor (which, as frequent and furtive glances in his direction informed her, seemed to consist primarily of allowing Lady Palmer to present him to all the county's most influential citizens—an elite group of which the Darringtons were not a part) and came to claim his dance.

Her fears were well founded. No sooner had James surrendered her to her next partner than Peregrine appeared at her side.

"My dance, I believe," he said, taking her elbow preparatory to leading her out onto the floor.

Young Mr. Christopher Higgins, newly arrived from Oxford for the sole purpose of waltzing with the belle of the district, bristled at this cavalier treatment.

"I believe you are mistaken, sir," Mr. Higgins protested. "This dance belongs to me."

Peregrine turned to Amanda. "Does it indeed?"

Amanda unfurled her fan and studied its thin wooden sticks, each of which bore the scrawled signature of one of her eager partners. "I fear Mr. Higgins is quite right, Mr. Palmer. In fact, all my dances appear to be taken."

He held out his hand. "Let me see."

Amanda surrendered her fan.

Peregrine studied the names. "Why, so they are."

Whereupon he closed the fan with a flick of his wrist and promptly snapped it in two, then handed the broken pieces to Mr. Higgins and led the sputtering Amanda back onto the dance floor.

"This—this passes all bounds, sir!" she cried, fairly quivering with outrage. "I shall expect you to replace my fan."

"I cannot think of anything that would give me greater pleasure," he declared, then frowned as he considered this pronouncement. "Actually I can, but I shall settle for a waltz, at least for the nonce. Come, Miss Amanda, admit you were equally at fault for giving away a dance you had already promised to me."

Amanda could not deny it, nor could she explain the impulse that had inspired her to commit such a breach of etiquette. Her instincts had undoubtedly been correct, however, for although she had found great enjoyment in whirling about the drawing room with her brother's tutor, she took no pleasure whatsoever in an exercise that made her feel light-headed and weak-kneed. Peregrine held her a precise and proper twelve inches away, but his hand at her waist burned through the thin muslin of her gown like a brand, a maddening mockery of a lover's embrace.

"Oh! You are insufferable! You are rude, and arrogant, and—and I don't know why you will persist in tormenting me! What have I ever done to you?"

"Why, only enchanted me, Ceres. Have I not said so?"

"Do not call me that! I am well aware that you must have met dozens of females far more enchanting than I. You see, I—I know who you are."

"Oh? Who am I?" Peregrine asked, grinning in anticipation of the insult he felt sure would follow.

"You may call yourself Mr. Palmer, but I know you to be the duke of Montford."

Peregrine froze in mid-step, causing another waltzing couple to careen into him. He stammered a disjointed apology to the glowering pair, then turned his attention back to Amanda. "*What* did you say?"

"I know you are the duke of Montford. I found your papers, you see. You left them in my basket."

Peregrine made no very comprehensible reply, merely muttered something under his breath.

"You do not deny it?" Amanda challenged.

"I can, and do! The very idea is preposterous."

Finding himself adjacent to the French windows opening onto the terrace, he deftly steered Amanda off the dance floor and out the door.

"Thank God for that, anyway! At least now we may talk undisturbed."

"You admit, then, that we have much to talk about," she said accusingly.

Peregrine gave a short, humorless laugh. "Oh, I'll admit that readily enough! I can see how you came to the conclusion you did, but I assure you I am not the duke of Montford. I am merely holding the papers for him until—well, until he requests that I return them."

Amanda's eyes narrowed in suspicion, but she could find no trace of mockery in his voice or manner. "I don't believe you," she said anyway, just in case.

Peregrine shrugged. "Believe anything you like, but believing me to be a duke will not make it so." He frowned. "Is it so very important to you—that I be a duke, I mean?"

Her gaze fell before his curiously intense expression. "I am sure it is nothing to me *what* you may be!" she retorted, tossing her golden head in a gesture somehow more indicative of pique than nonchalance.

"Oh, but it must be," chided Peregrine in quite his old manner. "How else are you to know how to style yourself once we are married?"

At this home question, whatever crushing rejoinder Amanda would have made died a-borning, leaving her to gape at her infuriating swain with bulging eyes and dropping jaw.

Peregrine, taking advantage of her unaccustomed silence, seized the opportunity to possess himself of her hands. "You will marry me, won't you? If you don't, I'm going to feel like an awful fool."

She made a half-hearted attempt to free her hands. "It would be no more than you deserve," she said, but her tone lacked conviction even to her own ears.

Peregrine, at any rate, was not deceived. He released her hands, but only so that he might take her into his arms. "My darling girl!"

After a prolonged and rather disjointed conversation, which would have been of interest to no one but themselves, Amanda bethought herself of the duke who had indirectly brought them together.

"Are you truly acquainted with the duke of Montford?"

"Indeed, I am—quite well, in fact."

"I can see you must be, if he would trust you to keep his papers for him, but why would he ask you to do such a thing?"

"He—er—he does not wish to be known as the duke just yet."

"This is famous!" cried Amanda, scenting an intrigue. "Is he here tonight?" She peered through the French windows over his shoulder, but could see nothing more fascinating than the sight of Mr. Fanshawe guiding her sister through the final movements of the waltz. "Oh, look! There is Meg. Won't she be shocked to learn I have found a husband all on my own, without ever setting foot in London!"

"You dislike London?"

"I have never been. I daresay it must be a very nice place to visit, but I should miss the people of Montford."

"Then I shall ask my uncle to give us the dower house, so that you need not be far from your family. Except for the honeymoon, of course, where I shall insist upon the strictest privacy!"

Amanda blushed so charmingly at this prospect that Peregrine felt compelled to kiss her again.

"Speaking of my uncle," he continued, having completed this exercise, "I'll see if I can roust him out of the card room. A toast is clearly in order, and his cellars must boast something worthy of the occasion."

With impassioned promises not to be separated from his betrothed for a moment longer than was strictly necessary, Peregrine took himself off in search of Sir Humphrey. Amanda gazed adoringly after the departing form of her betrothed until he was swallowed up in the crowd, then returned to the ballroom to seek out Margaret. She found her deep in conversation with Aunt Hattie and her erstwhile whist partner, Mrs. Emmeline Thornton.

"Who would have thought it?" Aunt Hattie exclaimed. "It was not dear Emmy who cheated me out of my ten shillings, but that dreadful Mrs. Blakeney!"

Her companion nodded, setting the plumes adorning her spangled turban aflutter. "Quite right, Miss Darrington. She tried the same thing with me—not once, mind you, but twice! Others have remarked upon it as well; in fact, between you and me and the lamppost, she has made herself *persona non grata* with the ladies' Wednesday afternoon ombre circle."

"And to think I might never have known had not Mr. Fanshawe insisted that she take his place at the card table," sighed Aunt Hattie.

"Indeed, yes! An old friendship might have been lost forever. Depend upon it, Hattie, it was a happy day when your family engaged that young man."

"Oh, Meg, is it not wonderful?" Amanda interrupted, giving her sister's arm an affectionate squeeze. "I am to be married!"

Margaret could not help smiling at her obvious delight. "Of course you are, my love! Why, you are the belle of Montford; you will have no trouble at all in finding an eligible husband. I shall not be surprised if you have all London at your feet by Easter."

Amanda laughed, a musical expression of such joy that it put the violins to shame. "No, silly! I have found an eligible husband right here in Montford. I am betrothed!"

Margaret's smile froze, and the blood slowly drained from her face.

Amanda, finding her sister less than ecstatic at this announcement, hastened to reassure her. "It may not be a brilliant match, at least not by Society's standards," she acknowledged, "but surely no one can fault the tone of his mind, or the nobility of his character, or the sweetness of his temperament."

It was unlikely that Peregrine could have recognized himself in this glowing description, so it was hardly surprising that Margaret supposed it to refer, not to the squire's nephew, but to quite another object.

"B-But," she stammered. "But he—"

"I know this comes as a surprise," Amanda continued, her radiant smile undimmed. "Truth to tell, it came as something of a surprise to me, also! But I am certain that once you have had time to grow accustomed to the idea, you will come to love him as a brother."

No, never! The thought burst upon her consciousness with such startling clarity that for one horrifying moment Margaret feared she had spoken the words aloud. But no, Amanda still stood there beaming at her as if she hadn't a care in the world.

"But dear, have you thought—"

She got no further, for at that moment Peregrine appeared bearing two crystal flutes, each filled with bubbly champagne.

"Ah, Miss Darrington! Or may I call you Margaret, since you are to be my sister? Surely Amanda has told you she has just made me the happiest of men? My uncle is to make an announcement momentarily."

As if on cue, Sir Humphrey stepped up onto the raised dais and raised his hands, motioning for silence. "Friends and neighbors," he intoned, "it appears we are to have a wedding in Montford. Miss Amanda Darrington has consented to marry my rackety nephew Peregrine, who I think we can all agree has done nothing at all to deserve so charming a bride."

In spite of his disparaging words, Sir Humphrey fairly swelled with pride, while Peregrine and Amanda preened as if they had just invented the institution of matrimony. A murmur of approving voices rose to a buzz, then became a roar that filled Margaret's head, leaving her dizzy and weak at the knees. Finding a glass of champagne in her hand without quite knowing how it got there, she raised it to her lips and downed it in a single gulp. The roar in her head subsided, but the unsteadiness remained.

"Miss Darrington?" A gentle yet firm hand gripped her elbow, and a soothing voice spoke somewhere over her head. "Are you quite all right?"

She recognized the voice at once. "Mr. Fanshawe! Yes, yes, I am all right, 'tis only the heat, and the—are you going to drink that?" Without waiting for an answer, she seized his champagne glass and tipped the sparkling liquid down her own throat.

"Perhaps a breath of fresh air is in order," he suggested, gesturing toward the same French windows through which Peregrine and Amanda had passed only moments earlier.

"No, no! I shall be fine, I assure you."

It was imperative that she not be alone with him until she had mastered her emotions. For her first thought upon hearing Sir Humphrey's announcement had not been concern for her family's future, or regret for the brilliant marriage that would never be, or even anger at Amanda's improvidence. No, it had been *relief*—overpowering, overwhelming relief that Mr. Fanshawe was not to be her brother. She needed a quiet moment in which to ponder the significance of this discovery.

She was not to have it, however. Heedless of her protests, James steered her out the door and onto the balcony. Neither one spoke for a long moment, during which Margaret avoided his gaze by staring fixedly at the moonlit garden beyond the parapet.

"I know what you are thinking," James said at last, breaking a silence that threatened to stretch on indefinitely. "Granted, it is not the brilliant match you had hoped for, but Perry is far from penniless. You may rest easy on that head."

After all she'd had to say on the subject of Amanda's marriage prospects, she could hardly admit that at the moment they were the least of her concerns. "They—they have not known one another for very long," she said.

"Perhaps not. Still, I have seen Perry in the throes of calf-love any number of times over the years, but never to my knowledge did he seriously entertain thoughts of matrimony until he met your sister. I believe he truly cares for her."

"And she obviously cares for him. How very odd! If anyone had asked me, I should have said she disliked him intensely."

James joined her at the parapet, folding his long frame forward until his elbows rested on the railing, from which vantage point he might have an unobstructed view of her profile. "Perhaps she mistook her own heart," he suggested. "I believe it happens sometimes. One forms a certain image of the sort of person one might conceive an attachment for, only to fall deeply in love with someone who bears no resemblance to that image at all. 'The heart has its reasons' and all that, you know."

Margaret's chin came up in a brave little show of humor. "One might suppose you to speak from experience, Mr. Fanshawe."

He neither confirmed nor denied the charge, but smiled at her in such a way that she was forced to turn her attention back to the moon-drenched gardens.

"And so Amanda is to be married," she said, determinedly returning the conversation to its original, and far less disturbing, subject. "I have been scraping and saving for her Season so long, it seems very strange to think it has all been in vain."

"Perhaps the funds might be used to send Philip to school instead."

"You would deny me my brother's company as well as my sister's? I should hardly know what to do with myself."

"In that case," he said thoughtfully, "perhaps it is time you stopped thinking of your family and thought for a moment about yourself. Is there nothing that *you* want to do? Something just for yourself, with no thought for the consequences?"

Margaret was never quite certain afterwards what possessed her. Perhaps it was the silvery moonlight bathing the garden below, or the candlelight streaming through the French windows that lit James's golden hair like a halo, or—it must be said—the quantity of champagne that she had consumed far too quickly. Whatever the reason, she gazed up at James and knew, without a doubt, what it was that she most wanted to do. Slowly, deliberately, she clutched the lapels of his shiny, too-short evening coat and leaned toward him, rising up on tiptoe until her lips met his.

She was in his arms in an instant, not the decorous clasp of the waltz, but a passionate embrace which molded their bodies together and bent her head back at an angle which should have been extremely uncomfortable, yet was somehow just right. Bride clothes, dowries, marriage settlements—they would all be there tomorrow, waiting, demanding her attention. Tonight there was only Mr. Fanshawe, his lips on hers and his arms holding her as if he would never let her go.

Like all good things, however, it had to come to an end. Sanity eventually reasserted itself, and she stepped backward out of his embrace.

"I—I beg your pardon," she stammered. "Pray forgive me. I should not have—"

"Miss Darrington—Margaret—"

He reached for her hand, but even as he captured it, the French window opened and a broad swath of light illuminated them like a beacon.

"*There* you are!" Aunt Hattie puffed. "I've been searching everywhere. Oh, Margaret, is it not too delightful? Dear Mr. Palmer's aunt—not Lady Palmer, but his *other* aunt, Lady Windhurst, his mama's sister, you know—has offered to bring out our Amanda this autumn during the Little Season, and will even sponsor her presentation at Court! And best of all—though perhaps I should not say such a thing, but you will know what I mean!—she intends to pay all the expenses as a betrothal gift! Oh, my love, it is almost like a miracle, is it not?"

"Yes," Margaret said softly, avoiding James's too-penetrating gaze. "Almost."

CHAPTER 12

It was, indeed, almost like a miracle—almost, but not quite. Surely miracles did not make one toss and turn in one's bed all night, tormented by thoughts of what might have been. Now, too late, Margaret realized why she had so strenuously objected to the idea of Mr. Fanshawe's making overtures toward her sister. Amanda must not marry Mr. Fanshawe because, Margaret now knew, Mr. Fanshawe must marry no one but herself. She had made a point of telling herself (and, indeed, anyone else who would listen) that she was only acting in her family's best interests, when all the while she was motivated by petty jealousy of the basest sort—that which seeks its own self-interests, all the while purporting to be for its object's Own Good.

Alas, honesty and self-awareness did not erase the fact that Mr. Fanshawe was as ineligible a husband for Margaret as ever he had been for Amanda. Worse, in fact, for now that Amanda had made her choice, it would be wicked to expect Mr. Palmer to support not only his bride, but her improvident sister and that sister's impoverished husband as well.

Amanda had made her choice . . . Was it possible that Margaret now faced the choice that would forever change her life? Could there have been something in the old gypsy woman's predictions after all? No, for if that were the case, Mr. Fanshawe would be the happy possessor of a fortune. It would be foolhardy in the extreme to set so much store by the ramblings of a gypsy soothsayer that one married a poor man for love, only to spend the rest of one's life waiting for a fortune that never materialized.

With the coming of dawn, she knew what she had to do. Abandoning all attempts at sleep, she dressed quickly in a drab gray gown that matched her mood, then went downstairs to the study, where she busied herself with a series of sums as the sun crept over the horizon and spilled across the windowsill. A soft sound made her look up, blinking in the unexpectedly bright morning light.

"I had a feeling I would find you here," James said, smiling as he entered the room.

The pen slipped from her hand, spattering tiny drops of ink over her calculations. "Mr. Fanshawe! Do come in. Sit—sit down."

He advanced farther into the room, but did not sit. "Miss Darrington, I—"

"I—I have good news—at least, I trust you will find it so," she plunged hastily into speech, her hands very busy among the papers littering the desk. "Philip is to go to school, just as you suggested. He is to begin at the start of the Michaelmas term. As for yourself, you need not fear for your own future, for you will have two weeks' wages as well as a letter of the very highest recommendation. I hope it will be useful to you in—in seeking employment elsewhere. You will no doubt wish to reach the Pig and Whistle in time to catch the early stage, so I shall have Philip drive you there in the trap immediately after breakfast."

James's smile faded. "You're sending me away." It was a statement, not a question.

"Surely you must agree that your services would be superfluous. You knew this would be the case when you urged me to send him to school."

"Yes, and you steadfastly resisted my entreaties. Forgive

me, Miss Darrington, but it seems very odd that you should decide to take my advice today, of all days. If your decision has anything to do with what happened between us last night, let me assure you—"

She raised a hand to forestall him. "About last night, Mr. Fanshawe, surely the less said, the better. Suffice it to say that it was a momentous occasion, with emotions running very close to the surface, and that my aunt's ratafia and mild claret cup were neither one of them sufficient to prepare me for the potency of Sir Humphrey's champagne."

James clasped his hands lightly behind his back and slowly began to pace the floor, just as if he were delivering a lecture on Latin or Greek. "There is an expression, Miss Darrington, which we find in Plato. Perhaps you are familiar with it: *in vino veritas.* Simply put, it means that when one is under the influence of alcohol, one is likely to say or do the things one wishes but hasn't the courage to do when sober."

"I am indeed familiar with the expression, Mr. Fanshawe, but I fear Mr. Plato and I are doomed to disagree on this point. In my experience—limited though it is—one is more likely to do things that would never even occur to one without, er, liquid stimulant."

"I am sorry to hear that," James said, although the blue eyes twinkling behind his spectacles looked anything but remorseful. "For I had been wanting to kiss you, too—wanting it for quite some time, as a matter of fact."

"Really, Mr. Fanshawe, this conversation is most improper—"

"Not at all. You have just given me notice, so I am no longer in your employ. I am merely a private gentleman asking a lady if she will do me the honor of—"

Margaret clapped her hands over her ears, shutting out

156

the question she knew she must refuse. "I beg you, sir, say no more! I daresay you feel an obligation to offer for me after our—indiscretion—of last night, but—"

"Surely you cannot think I would make you an offer for such a reason as that!" exclaimed James, suddenly serious. "As a matter of fact, Miss Darrington, I find an uncommon delight in your company, and flattered myself that my feelings were reciprocated."

"You must know that the idea of any marriage between us is quite impossible!"

"Am I to understand, then, that you do *not* feel for me that degree of—of affection which I feel for you?"

She smiled sadly. "I fear our feelings have very little to say to the matter. Love in a cottage may sound very well in novels, but it has nothing to do with real life. You are in no position to support a wife, and I cannot—*will* not!—be dependent upon my sister and Mr. Palmer."

"Tell me, Miss Darrington, would my suit be as objectionable to you if I were the duke of Montford?"

She blinked at him. "What sort of question is that?"

He shook his head, waving away the words he had not meant to say. "Never mind. You have given your answer, and there is nothing more to be said. I suppose, then, that this must be goodbye."

It was precisely what she had intended, and yet she was suddenly and perversely reluctant to see him go. "I—I would not wish to appear ungrateful for everything you have done for us," she said, holding out her hand to him. "I am sure Philip and—and indeed all of us—will—will miss you very much."

Much to her chagrin, he took her hand and, raising it to his lips, pressed a lingering kiss into her palm. Of their own volition, her fingers curled to cup his cheek.

"And so shall I miss all of you. Goodbye, Miss Darrington. Please accept my sincerest wishes for your every happiness."

A more public leave-taking occurred later that morning, after James's bags were packed and loaded onto the trap which would soon convey him to the Pig and Whistle. He made a very pretty farewell speech thanking them all for binding his wounds and taking him to their collective bosom. All the while, Aunt Hattie wept silently into her handkerchief and the younger Darringtons cast faintly accusing glances in Margaret's direction, as if they were certain that there was more to Mr. Fanshawe's abrupt departure than Philip's education. James then wished Amanda joy in her marriage, admonished Philip to mind his studies, kissed Aunt Hattie's damp cheek, and finally turned to Margaret. Her breath caught in her throat when he took her hand, and when he merely held it for a moment in a firm clasp, she hardly knew whether to be sorry or glad.

"Goodbye, Miss Darrington," he said. "Thank you again for all you have done for me."

He climbed aboard the trap, and Philip snapped the reins. The vehicle lurched into motion, and the Darrington ladies gradually dispersed to their usual activities—except for Margaret, who stood on the front stoop watching until the trap and its passengers disappeared over the hill.

Having nowhere else to go, James took the first stage to London, where he called upon his (or rather the duke of Montford's) solicitor. His reappearance rivaled that of the Prodigal.

"Your Grace!" exclaimed Mr. Mayhew, emerging from behind his massive desk to clasp James's hand in both of his own and pump it with enthusiasm. "May I say, sir, how good it is to see your Grace looking so very well? When you never arrived at Montford Park, I confess to fearing the worst."

"Your fears were very nearly realized, Mr. Mayhew," confessed James, submitting with a good grace to the solicitor's assault on his person. "In fact, I was set upon by footpads and temporarily deprived of my memory—ironically enough, not more than a couple of miles from the ducal lands. To make a long story short, I have spent the last few months teaching Latin to one of the local lads, scion of a family by the name of Darrington."

Mr. Mayhew pondered the name. "Darrington, Darrington—ah, yes! The Darrington property borders your own. An old and respected County family, but no money there, more's the pity. Won't they stare when they make their bows to their exalted neighbor, only to discover that the duke and the Latin tutor are one and the same?"

James's expression grew wooden. "I have no plans to meet any of the local gentry anytime soon. I expect to remain fixed in Town for most of the year."

"Your Grace was displeased with the house?" Mr. Mayhew asked in some consternation, as if he was personally responsible for its failure to delight.

"No, no, how could anyone be displeased with it? Suffice it to say the district holds—unpleasant associations."

Mr. Mayhew nodded in sympathy. "Indeed, one can see how it might." The solicitor was obviously thinking of the attack, and James saw no need to disabuse him of the notion. "No doubt these unhappy memories will fade with time. But until then, sir, the estate—"

"I shall employ a bailiff to administer the estate."

"Very good, your Grace. I shall request an employment

agency to send 'round a list of qualified candidates. In the meantime, I have taken the liberty of staffing the town house against your Grace's arrival. Not a large staff, mind you, only a butler, a cook, a groom, two footmen, and two chambermaids. Your Grace will naturally wish to choose his own valet."

James thought this an appalling waste, and said so. "I have been dressing myself for twenty-seven years," he observed. "It is unlikely I shall forget how at this late date."

Mr. Mayhew did not argue the point, but he flicked a pained glance at James's shabby clothing. "On a related subject, your Grace, I am charged with messages from the earl of Torrington, begging that you will call upon him as soon as possible after your arrival in Town."

At any other time, James might have inquired as to this seeming *non sequitur,* but the mention of his friend from University days drove such irrelevancies from his mind. "Torrington? To be sure I will! I haven't seen old Torry since we were at school together."

Armed with Lord Torrington's direction, James set out for his friend's rooms in the Albany. He found the earl, a lithe young man with a head of chestnut curls arranged in careful disarray, studying his reflection in the pier glass as he put the finishing touches to a cravat of magnificent design. Upon observing James's entrance through the glass, his sartorial efforts were forgotten, and he whirled around to greet his visitor.

"James, is it you at last? Are you aware that your disappearance has been the talk of London for the last two months and more?"

James, advancing into the room, submitted to being pounded heartily upon the back. "Disappearance? Nonsense, Torry! I've known where I was all along. Well, almost all along," he amended hastily, treating Torrington to an expurgated version of his adventures in which Miss Darrington's name figured not at all. "But look at you! What a dandy you've become! What do call those absurd breeches?"

"Trousers, my boy, Petersham trousers," Torrington corrected him, stepping back so that his friend might enjoy an unobstructed view of striped leggings cut full from hip to ankle, where they were gathered into a flounce. "The very last word, I assure you!"

"Good Lord, let us hope so!" said James fervently, his dimpled grin robbing the words of any insult.

"You should be the last person to criticize anyone else's wardrobe," the maligned dandy retorted without heat. "Whoever heard of a duke going about in rags? I must introduce you to my tailor."

"And be turned out in—what did you call them?—Petersham trousers? No, I thank you!"

"No indeed—haven't the figure for it, my lad. Too long and spindly by half!"

"Well, thank God for that," said James, unoffended.

Over the days that followed, the duke and the earl were forever in one another's company, the latter being determined to initiate the former into the pleasures of the aristocratic life. Under Torrington's auspices, James was measured and fitted for a new wardrobe by Weston and beaten (he said) to a bloody pulp by the famed pugilist Gentleman Jackson. He played cards at White's, bid on horseflesh at Tattersall's, and tested his marksmanship at Manton's shooting gallery. He dined at the Pulteney, strolled in Hyde Park, and attended the theater at both Covent Garden and Drury Lane. Through it all, however, there remained an ache in his heart and an emptiness in his soul that no diversion could entirely banish.

And then, three weeks after his arrival in London, he was formally presented to the House of Lords, to whom he delivered his maiden speech.

It could not be said that this oratorical exercise was an unqualified success. As curate of Fairford parish, James had often had reason to deplore his tendency to stammer out his sermons and, faced with so August an audience as the assembled Lords, he was not surprised when this tendency reasserted itself with a vengeance. Moreover, his topic—education for the masses—was still several years ahead of its time. Still, the romantic story of his disappearance already inclined most people in his favor, and to this were added the not inconsiderable charms of a modest demeanor and a self-deprecating wit. When, in the middle of his speech, the Dowager Marchioness of Worthington—as high a stickler as had ever adorned the Visitor's Gallery—demanded in quite an audible whisper, "Who *is* that charming boy?" James's success was assured. By nightfall, the new duke of Montford was the darling of London.

If further evidence of his triumph were required, it arrived the next morning. James was enjoying the unaccustomed luxury of lingering over breakfast when his new butler entered the room bearing a silver tray piled high with letters.

"What's all this?" James asked, setting down his coffee cup.

"The morning post, your Grace," the butler intoned, laying his burden on the table at James's elbow.

"Thank you—Reese, is it?"

"Reeves, your Grace."

"I beg your pardon," said James with a singularly sweet smile. "I assure you, I shall learn it eventually."

"I am sure your Grace has more important matters to occupy his mind," the butler replied in a tone so damping that James somehow felt he was somehow at fault for deeming his servants worthy of being called by their proper names. He caught himself up before he could beg the butler's pardon again, and turned his attention to opening and reading the morning's mail.

He was still engaged in this task when Lord Torrington burst upon him, dressed for riding in form-fitting buckskins and top-boots. "Saddle up that pretty little hack you purchased at Tatt's, and let us away to the park. Your public awaits! Hallo, what's all this?"

"Invitations," said James, looking up at him with an expression of comic dismay. "Invitations from people I don't know, to functions I can't identify. What, pray, is a rout-party, and do I want to go to one?"

"Rather depends on who's giving it. Here, let me see." Torrington twitched the letter from James's hand and studied the spidery script. "Rigsby woman. Run, dear boy, run! Four unmarried daughters, each one homelier than the one before. What else do you have there?"

One by one, Torrington worked his way through the heap of correspondence. "Card party at the lodgings of Mr. Richard Brantley-Hughes? Bad *ton*, my lad! Probably hoping to put the touch on you for money. By all means, stay away! Soirée given by Mr. and Mrs. Benjamin Beamish? Mushrooms, both of 'em. Avoid like the plague."

"But Torry, who are all these people, and why are they writing to me?"

"Toad-eaters one and all, hoping to bask in your reflected glory."

"My—*what* glory? Good Lord, I haven't any!"

"You may not have had yesterday, but since your appearance before the House of Lords, you are the Toast of London. All Mayfair is clamoring for a glimpse of you."

James grimaced. "No doubt they are curious to see a stammering yokel in the flesh."

"Balderdash! Society, in its infinite wisdom, has pronounced you delightfully unaffected, therefore delightfully unaffected you are—at least until Society decrees otherwise. Enjoy it while you may—notoriously fickle, Society."

James opened his mouth to protest, but found no words in English or any of the classical tongues that adequately expressed his astonishment.

Lord Torrington, oblivious to his friend's struggle, returned his attention to the stack of invitations. "Let us see, whom shall you honor with your presence tonight? Ah! Lord and Lady Holbrook are giving a ball. Excellent *ton*, you know, and the diamond of the Season is very likely to be in attendance. Want to dip your oar in before someone else snaps her up—although, unless rumor lies, she's already rebuffed three barons, two baronets, five mere 'misters,' and a viscount."

James's expression grew wooden. "I don't think of matrimony, Torry."

"My dear boy, whoever said you must? Believe me, every marriageable female in England will have more than enough opinion on the subject for you both."

Prior to the Holbrook ball, all James's public appearances had been limited to the daylight hours, since his new evening wear had not yet been delivered. As for the garments he had worn to Lady Palmer's entertainment in Montford, Lord Torrington had taken one look at them and promptly consigned them to the fire. As James had watched the flames leaping and dancing over them, he could not help feeling somehow that those magical moments in which he had held Miss Darrington in his arms were somehow being consumed as well.

In any case, he had put those memories resolutely behind him, and placed himself in the hands of his new valet, a capable man by the name of Doggett, who possessed the curious habit of referring to himself and his master as if they were a single unit. This individual buzzed about James like a particularly energetic bumblebee, now coaxing stiff folds of starched cambric into a *cravate Sentimentale,* now easing the form-fitting coat over James's shoulders.

"There!" he pronounced at last. "We are finished!" With these words, he stepped aside so that James might admire his handiwork.

James turned to his looking glass, and found himself staring into the gaze of a stranger. His guinea-gold curls had been stylishly cropped and brushed until they shone, one lock falling artlessly over his high forehead. His dark-blue evening coat (unlike the one so ruthlessly burned by the earl) possessed sleeves long enough to cover his wrists, while the discreet use of buckram wadding in the shoulders rendered his physique less lanky. His narrow waist, encompassed about by a waistcoat of ivory-colored brocade, needed no lacing to achieve the fashionably wasp-waisted silhouette, while his black stockinette pantaloons clung to his legs like a second skin.

"Good Lord!" said James with a shaky laugh. "I look a regular popinjay!"

"If we may be forgiven for saying so," put in the valet, "we find ourselves to look particularly distinguished."

"Yes, you've done very well, considering what you have been given to work with. Thank you, Doggett. That will be all."

The valet began to gather up the tools of his trade, then turned back to his master. "There is one other thing, if we may be so bold. Mr. Mayhew requested that we give this to your Grace. It has been worn by the dukes of Montford for generations."

He opened his outstretched hand to reveal a large sapphire set in a gold mount. James slid the ring onto his finger, and for the first time felt a sense of connection to his unknown forebears.

"It is the largest of a set of matching sapphires in your Grace's possession," Doggett continued. "The remaining stones comprise a parure of a necklace, bracelet, and earrings. These are usually given to each new duchess upon her marriage, as a wedding gift from her husband."

"*Et tu, Brute?*" James asked, wincing.

"Beg pardon, your Grace?" asked the valet, bewildered.

James shook his head. "Never mind."

CHAPTER 13

If James suspected Lord Torrington of exaggerating his new-found celebrity, five minutes in the Holbrook ballroom was sufficient to inform him that, if anything, his friend had understated the case. James was still in the act of thanking his host and hostess for their kind invitation when he was beset by a hoard of fashionably dressed strangers, all begging Lady Holbrook for an introduction. Her ladyship was happy to oblige, to the point that James, struggling valiantly to match names with faces, could not have identified with certainty more than a half-dozen of his fellow guests within half an hour of making their acquaintance. Eventually, however, amongst the host of unfamiliar names and equally unfamiliar faces, there was spoken a name he knew, a face which had once filled his every waking moment, and haunted his dreams at night.

"—And this," said her ladyship, ushering forward an uncommonly lovely young lady in palest pink, "is Miss Cynthia Prescott. Miss Prescott, his Grace, the duke of Montford."

She looked exactly as he remembered her. Oh, her dark hair was more fashionably styled, and she had thrown off the demure muslins of the rural beauty for the silks and satins of the modish debutante, but in all other ways, all ways that mattered, she was unchanged. He was surprised that this should be so; he had thought she must look older in some way. So very much had happened to him since he had last seen her that it seemed much longer than the mere four months it was.

"Your Grace." Miss Prescott sank into a deep curtsy. "The duke and I were acquainted once upon a time, Lady Holbrook, although he has grown so fine I doubt he still remembers me."

"Remember you?" James echoed. "Of course I do! How could I forget you?"

"Very prettily said, your Grace," nodded Lady Holbrook, beaming her approval.

"Oh, listen!" cried Miss Prescott. "The musicians have struck up the waltz. Do you recall how we used to waltz in Fairford, your Grace?"

"Indeed, I do," said James, quick to take his cue. "Will you do me the honor?"

He offered his arm and Miss Prescott, smiling shyly up at him, placed her gloved hand upon it. As he led her onto the floor, a buzz of conversation followed them.

"—What a striking a couple they make!"

"—No hope for the rest of us, not now that Montford has thrown his hat into the ring."

"—Old acquaintances, I hear. Unfair advantage, that, what?"

Oblivious to it all, James was aware only of a pair of large, bright eyes sparkling up at him in a way that Miss Darrington's never had. Nor, for that matter, had Miss Darrington ever clung to his arm as if he were her one hope of heaven. The invitation in Miss Prescott's gaze was as a balm to his bruised heart. He would know better, this time, than to take her overtures seriously. He would demonstrate to Miss Prescott, and to the world, that he was no longer a naïve curate wearing his heart on his sleeve; he was the duke of Montford, and he could play the game with the best of them.

"Tell me, Miss Prescott, what do you think of London?" he asked, settling his arm about her waist as the dance commenced.

"Oh, I like it very well."

"And it obviously likes you."

She peeped up at him through her lashes. "Everyone has been very kind to a simple country girl."

"A 'simple country girl'?" James echoed in skeptical accents. "Doing it much too brown, Miss Prescott. Surely you cannot be speaking of the belle of Fairford!"

They fell into reminiscences of village life, and while neither was tactless enough to mention James's unsuccessful courtship, both were very much aware of their shared history. The memory lent a certain poignancy to the intimacy of the waltz.

"But what of you, Mr. Weather—oh, I beg your pardon! Of course I should say your Grace! How do you find the Metropolis?"

"Terrifying," replied James without hesitation. "My butler scares me to death."

Miss Prescott laughed aloud at this sally, a tinkling, musical laugh that made more than one head turn to regard her with mingled admiration, envy, and regret. She was still laughing when James led her off the floor, and her cheeks were charmingly flushed—whether from laughter, the exertions of the dance, or something else, only she and her partner knew for certain.

Her father was waiting with her mother against the wall to receive her, word of his daughter's triumph having reached him in the card room.

"Mama, Papa, what do you think?" cried Miss Prescott gaily. "The poor duke is being shockingly bullied by his butler. Do tell him he must escape the fellow for one evening, and dine with us!"

Sir Reginald Prescott was much struck with this suggestion. "Dashed if that ain't a fine notion! You come and take your mutton with us, your Grace."

"Yes, pray join us for dinner one evening next week—shall we say Thursday?" seconded Lady Prescott.

"Won't be like it's the first time. His Grace was forever underfoot at our place in Fairford," Sir Reginald added as an aside to anyone within hearing. "Always knew he was destined for great things even then, didn't we, puss?"

"Of course, Papa," agreed Miss Prescott, tucking her gloved hand more securely into the crook of James's elbow.

"Pray step back, Lady Holbrook, I beg you," beseeched James, laughing. "Miss Prescott and her father are telling such bald-faced lies, I fear a lightning bolt may strike at any moment. In truth, the Prescotts knew me as a parish curate with nothing to recommend me but a modest talent for the violin."

"So you are a musician!" exclaimed Mrs. Dunworthy, hovering nearby in the hopes of maneuvering the duke into dancing with her daughter, a thin, sandy-haired girl with an unfortunate tendency to blend into the wall. "I am hosting a musical evening on Monday next. Do say you will come and favor us with a song!"

James quickly demurred, but was obliged to consent to attend the Dunworthys' musical evening, dine with the Prescotts, and solicit Miss Dunworthy for the supper dance before he was able to make good his escape.

It may be that this last displeased Miss Prescott, or perhaps she had not yet been in London long enough to learn discretion. Whatever the reason, when after supper she found herself alone with Miss Dunworthy in the retiring room set aside for the ladies, that damsel's singing of the duke's praises touched a raw nerve.

"Is he not the most agreeable gentleman of all your acquaintance?" Miss Dunworthy enthused. "Only fancy! He promised to come to Mama's musical evening, and said he looked forward to hearing me play my new sonata."

Miss Prescott, occupied in the application of lip rouge to her rosebud mouth, cast a disdainful look at her companion's reflection in the looking glass. "He was always polite, even before he became a duke," she conceded with a marked lack of enthusiasm.

"You knew him before?" asked Miss Dunworthy, agog with curiosity. "Were you well acquainted?"

"Very well indeed! In fact—" She broke off, eyes demurely downcast. "But I must say no more upon that head."

"What? Oh, what?"

"You must never tell another living soul," commanded Miss Prescott.

"No, never!" breathed Miss Dunworthy.

Miss Prescott took her hand and squeezed it confidingly. "In fact, he once asked me to marry him."

"Never say you turned him down!"

"What else could I do? He was quite shockingly poor in those days, you know. My father would never have countenanced such a match," she added, relishing the rôle of romantic heroine.

"And now? Does he still love you, do you suppose?"

Miss Prescott lowered her eyes with maidenly modesty. "I'm sure I couldn't say."

To her chagrin, she realized it was true. Certainly their waltz had been all that was agreeable, and he had paid her several very pretty compliments. And yet this in itself was disturbing, for there had been none of the blushing and

171

stammering that had characterized his courtship before. Surely his utter lack of constraint must argue against a heart so deeply engaged as it once had been.

Miss Prescott thrust this unpleasant thought from her mind. She had captivated him once; she could do so again. Turning back to the mirror, she pinched her cheeks to give them a rosy blush, then sallied forth to conquer.

As for Miss Dunworthy, she was a very loyal girl, and so overcome was she at becoming the confidante of the Peerless Miss Prescott that, had the other young people present been at all kind to her, she very likely would have taken the secret to her grave. But later in the evening, finding herself alone and ignored in the midst of a merry group of persons her own age, Miss Dunworthy saw the opportunity to be, for once in her short life, the cynosure of all eyes. And so, when there came a brief lull in the conversation, she hesitated only for a moment before plunging into speech.

"Did you know," she said to the group at large in a nervous, high-pitched tone, "that Miss Prescott and the duke of Montford were once almost engaged to be married?"

James arrived at the Prescotts' rented lodgings the following Thursday fully expecting to be one of a number of dinner guests. Great was his surprise when the butler ushered him to the drawing room and he found himself alone with the family.

"Ah, your Grace!" exclaimed Mrs. Prescott, gliding forward to greet him. "Always such an excellent young man—so very prompt!"

Even to James's untrained eye, her demi-trained gown of spangled satin over gauze seemed a bit overdone for a quiet family dinner. The same might be said for Miss Prescott's ensemble, whose yards of celestial blue satin and silver lamé seemed more suited to presentation at Court than dining with an old friend. As he was by no means an authority on ladies' clothing, however, he dismissed the fanciful thought and, upon hearing the dinner gong sound, offered his hostess his arm.

One glimpse of the dining room was sufficient to inform him that, however small the guest list, this was no casual family dinner. To be sure, all the leaves had been removed from the gleaming mahogany table, but the abbreviated surface that remained was all but obliterated beneath settings of gilt-rimmed china, sparkling crystal, gleaming silver, and starched linen napery.

"I—I'm not worthy of such magnificence," said James, blinking.

"Nonsense, my boy!" protested Mr. Prescott, taking his place at the head of the shortened table. "Nothing's too good for our duke, you know."

Mrs. Prescott, seated opposite her husband, seconding this assessment, added, "You might have knocked me over with a feather when Mr. Bainbridge—you do remember Mr. Bainbridge, the vicar?—when Mr. Bainbridge wrote to tell us the news."

"I remember Mr. Bainbridge very well. Tell me, how does he go on?"

"Oh, very well, very well indeed," Mrs. Prescott assured him, dismissing the vicar with a wave of her bejeweled hand. "But do tell us about your holdings in Montford, your Grace. Mr. Bainbridge was under the impression they are quite extensive."

Mr. Prescott drank deeply from his wineglass, then wiped his mouth on his sleeve. "I'll wager they bring in a tidy sum in rents, what?"

James found himself extremely reluctant to discuss so

personal a subject, especially with footmen milling about the table pouring wine into goblets and ladling soup into bowls from a large tureen. He sought refuge in a reply that was at once evasive and entirely honest. "Truth to tell, I hardly know. The accident, you know, interrupted my visit, so I have not yet had an opportunity to view the property for myself. But do tell me all the news from Fairford! How go the squire and his lady, and young Thomas?"

Seeing his wife glaring at him from the other end of the table, Mr. Prescott tucked one corner of his napkin into the neckband of his shirt. "Nice to see you haven't forgotten your friends, anyway."

"Indeed yes," agreed Mrs. Prescott. "And so very gracious of you not to hold a grudge against our poor chick for—"

"Mama!" urged Miss Prescott *sotto voce* from her seat opposite James.

"Well you know for what, so there's no use my repeating it. Although your kind attentions to our little Cynthia at Lady Holbrook's ball were such that I wanted to weep!"

James, by this time thoroughly uncomfortable with the direction of the conversation, was prompted by some demon to beg his hostess's pardon. "Had I known my dancing with Miss Prescott would have so unhappy a result, I should have yielded my place to another."

"No, no!" Mrs. Prescott protested. "I'm sure I never meant that! It is only when I think of the pain you must have suffered—"

"In that case, ma'am, let me set your mind at ease. Your daughter was quite right to give me the answer she did. One has only to see her in her proper setting, surrounded by beaux, to know she would have been wasted on a village curate."

Across the table, Miss Prescott turned quite pink with pleasure, while Mrs. Prescott exhaled a blissful sigh. "Very prettily said, your Grace."

"Ah, but you're not a village curate anymore," Mr. Prescott pointed out.

"Very true, sir, but neither is she merely the belle of Fairford. It appears that we were both destined for bigger and, let us hope, better things."

Assuming that Miss Prescott's embarrassment at her parents' machinations must exceed even his own, James cast a glance of sympathetic understanding in her direction, only to experience a rude awakening. Miss Prescott's head was modestly bowed, but she smiled coyly up at him through her long, curling lashes.

James's hackles rose. He was forcibly reminded of the annual Fairford Christmas Hunt, in which Mr. Prescott was an avid participant, and wondered if this was how the unfortunate fox felt. The Prescotts' intentions could not have been plainer if the butler had met him at the door with the huntsman's cry of "view halloo!"

This, then, was what it was like to be courted for one's wealth and position. This was the sort of behavior of which he had believed Miss Darrington capable. Good God! He must have been mad. Her pride—the same pride that would not allow her to marry a poor man and then sponge off her sister—would prevent her from behaving in so brazen a manner. Unfortunately, he had not the luxury of pondering in what other ways he might have wronged Miss Darrington; one moment's inattention, he feared, and he might find himself betrothed willy-nilly to Miss Prescott.

His worst fears were confirmed after dinner, when the ladies excused themselves from the table.

"Now that it's just you and me," said Mr. Prescott, dispensing port into two glasses with a liberal hand, "we can talk business—dowries and jointures and such. I'll wager my Cynthia's portion won't be a drop in the bucket to you, but—"

"Sir, I fear you are laboring under a misapprehension," James protested. "Your daughter rejected my proposal—quite decisively, in fact."

"Pshaw! I shouldn't set too much store by that, if I were you. Maidenly modesty, you know—"

"As I recall," continued James with a trace of the old bitterness, "she laughed in my face."

"Aye, I'll not deny she always was a foolish, flighty puss. But a Season in London has smoothed out the rough edges, don't you know. If you were to ask her again, I'll wager you would receive a very different response."

Of that much James was certain—certain enough, at any rate, to know he had no desire to put it to the test. "I had rather show Miss Prescott the courtesy of taking her at her word," he said in a haughty tone that would have made his ancestors proud. "Now, if you will excuse me, sir, I must make my farewells to the ladies. I must not be late for another engagement."

Although James contrived to make it through dinner without entanglement, he was less sure how to distance himself from a connection the Prescotts seemed determined to exploit. Common courtesy demanded that he call the next morning to thank Mrs. Prescott for her hospitality, and it would have been rude in the extreme not to join the family in their opera box when they had gone to the trouble of saving a seat for him. Likewise, to neglect standing up with Miss Prescott for the waltz at Almack's would have given rise to just the sort of vulgar speculation he most wished to avoid.

The *ton*, of course, knew nothing of his dilemma. They knew only that the duke of Montford and the divine Miss Prescott were constantly in one another's company. The romantically minded whispered of young love torn apart long ago by parental ambition; the less charitable observed that Miss Prescott must feel a pretty fool, having unwittingly whistled a duke down the wind. On one thing, however, all were agreed: an Interesting Announcement was surely imminent.

Such was the social climate when, in early October, the Misses Darrington arrived in London.

While it could not be said that Margaret looked forward to the trip with anything approaching her sister's eagerness, she was more than ready for a change of scenery. Every room of her beloved childhood home now seemed somehow empty without a certain male presence, and every autumn breeze seemed to whisper his name. As she helped Aunt Hattie pack Philip's bags for school, Margaret could not help wondering where Mr. Fanshawe was, and whether he had found other employment. Even the plans for Amanda's wedding lost much of their charm, accompanied as they were by a mocking voice in Margaret's head that chided, *It might have been you . . .*

It was somehow fittingly ironic that, having been at last banished from Margaret's girlhood fantasies by a far less eligible (and yet somehow infinitely more appealing) alternate, the name upon all of London's lips should be that of the duke of Montford.

"His disappearance and apparent resurrection from the dead have made him the talk of Society," explained their hostess, Peregrine's aunt Windhurst, as the sisters prepared for their maiden visit to Almack's. "Add to that his very marked courtship of the Season's most celebrated beauty—although there are those who say the Beauty is courting him—and you have all the makings of an *on dit*."

"Oh, is the duke to be married, then?" asked Amanda, fastening a string of milky white pearls about her slender neck. "Think of it, Meg, Montford Priory will have a mistress at last."

"I can think only that it might have been you," retorted Margaret with a smile. "Depend upon it, the duke will be beside himself when he sees what an opportunity he has lost."

"Does it still bother you that I am not to make a brilliant match?" asked Amanda, slipping her arm about Margaret's waist.

Margaret returned her sister's embrace. "All that matters is that you are happy," she said, and tried hard to believe it. "My only regret is that you are to leave me, just like Philip, and I shall be left all alone."

"You will still have Aunt Hattie," Amanda pointed out with the brutal candor of youth.

"Miss Darrington may well make a match of her own," put in Lady Windhurst. "Depend upon it, there are many gentlemen who have no desire to wed a chit from the schoolroom."

Margaret smiled, but made no reply. She had rebuffed one such gentleman during her own Season, and might have had offers from a few others, had she given them the least encouragement. Alas, she'd had no desire to marry them then, and she had even less desire to do so now, when they must forever fall short of a certain tutor of her acquaintance.

At last the final ribbon was tied and the final curl pinned into place. In no time at all, Peregrine was at the door, ready to escort his ladies to that pinnacle of social heights, Almack's.

"I am sure you both remember the rules," said Lady Windhurst, enumerating them nonetheless. "The doors close promptly at eleven, and no one—not even the hero of Waterloo, Wellington himself—will be admitted after that time. You may stand up for any of the country dances, but do not accept any gentleman's invitation to waltz unless you have been granted permission from one of the patronesses. Oh, and speaking of patronesses, be sure to express your gratitude to Lady Jersey, who granted your vouchers."

Once inside the hallowed portals, the Darrington sisters were surprised to find their surroundings so very ordinary. Lady Palmer's ballroom had been more ornately decorated than the rather austere King Street establishment. But if the rooms themselves were somewhat plain, the occupants more than made up for the lack of ostentation. Here were elegant dandies with shirt-points so high they could scarcely turn their heads, military men whose bright red coats bristled with medals, blushing damsels in demure white muslin, and dashing young matrons in daring *décolletage*.

"Pray, Lady Windhurst, who is *that?*" Amanda asked.

Although Amanda was far too well bred to point, Margaret had no difficulty in identifying the object of her curiosity. Across the room, a dark-haired vision in primrose yellow laughed up into the adoring gazes of a cluster of admiring gentlemen. The radiance of her smile was such that all eyes were drawn to her like moths to a flame.

"That is Miss Cynthia Prescott," her ladyship replied.

"Known in certain circles as the Peerless Miss Prescott," added Peregrine.

"And, did they but know it, the gentlemen buzzing about her like so many honeybees are wasting their time," her ladyship continued. "Miss Prescott is rumored to be on the verge of becoming betrothed to the duke of Montford."

"Only fancy, Meg, she might soon be our neighbor! Which one do you suppose is the duke?" Amanda inquired eagerly, standing on tiptoe for a better look.

"Er, hadn't we better dance?" Peregrine put in hastily. "The next set is about to form."

"Yes, yes, in a minute." Amanda patted her fiancé's arm placatingly. "First I want to see the duke."

Lady Windhurst scanned the crowd about Miss Prescott. "His Grace is—" She frowned, finding no sign of him. "It appears his Grace is not in attendance tonight. He is not usually difficult to spot, for he stands quite half a head taller than anyone else in the room."

Margaret, watching as the Beauty laughed and flirted with her court, felt the last of her dreams shatter into a thousand pieces. What folly, to think that any man capable of attaching such loveliness would ever look twice at anything rural Montford had to offer! What a fool she had been! Her plans for salvaging her family's fortunes had been doomed from the start.

James, his shaking fingers struggling to coax his cravat into a waterfall knot, made one false move and inadvertently wrecked the work of the last quarter-hour. Ripping the creased strip of linen from his neck, he muttered a word he would never have spoken from the Fairford pulpit, and felt instantly ashamed of himself. Had the duke already banished the curate so completely?

"If we may be excused for saying so," his plural valet interposed, "the doors of Almack's will be shut at eleven, and it is already more than half past ten."

"Thank you, Doggett, we are—that is, I am well aware

180

of the time," said James, reaching for yet another cravat to mangle.

"His Grace appears somewhat restless this evening," observed the valet, displaying a hitherto unsuspected talent for understatement. "Perhaps we may be of some assistance?"

Much as it galled James to admit that, after twenty-seven years, he was suddenly incapable of dressing himself, he could not dispute the evidence of his own reflection in the looking glass. He surrendered the cravat into his valet's capable hands without protest.

"Very good, your Grace," pronounced this individual, beaming with approval. "We shall have you ready in a trice. If we may be so bold, we would not wish to disappoint Miss Prescott, would we?"

In point of fact, it was not Miss Prescott who was uppermost in James's mind. It was, if the valet had only known, a certain card that had been delivered with the afternoon post. This billet, scrawled in Peregrine's untidy hand, informed James of that young man's arrival in Town only that afternoon and indicated his intention of calling upon James the next day, as that evening would find him occupied in escorting his betrothed to Almack's.

And where Amanda went, James reasoned, Margaret would very likely follow. . . .

He arrived at Almack's a scant five minutes before eleven, and was welcomed effusively by no less a personage than Lady Jersey herself.

"Fie on you, your Grace, for keeping us waiting so long!" she chided, bearing down upon him with ostrich plumes bobbing in her hair. "Poor Miss Prescott has been cooling her heels since nine o'clock. You had best have a care, or someone else will take advantage of your negligence and snatch her away. Shall I take you to her?"

"In a moment," replied James, scanning the crowd from his superior height. "First I should like you to introduce me to that young lady there."

Lady Jersey craned her neck in an effort to follow his gaze. "Which one?"

"Right there, the one talking to Lady Windhurst."

"Ah, the Darrington girl! Very well, your Grace, but I must warn you that she is already betrothed."

"No, no, not Miss Amanda. The other—her sister."

The room was filled to overflowing, but such was Lady Jersey's influence that a word here, a tap of her fan there, and the crowd parted before them. At last James stood near enough to his erstwhile employer that he might have reached out and touched her.

"Miss Darrington," said the patroness, "may I present the duke of Montford, who is eager to make your acquaintance?"

Margaret turned with a swirl of ivory satin, and froze. Every drop of color drained from her face as she took in every detail of his changed appearance, from his stylishly cropped golden hair to the kid-leather pumps on his feet.

"Miss Darrington," he said, taking her gloved hand. Then, just before touching his lips to her cold fingers, he unwittingly sealed his fate. He winked.

"Forgive me, Lady Jersey," Margaret said in a steady yet expressionless voice quite unlike her own, "but I must beg to be excused. I find I have no desire for the duke's acquaintance."

And so saying, she snatched her hand from James's grasp and fled the room.

CHAPTER 14

Twelve hours later, Margaret sat slump-shouldered in Lady Windhurst's sunny breakfast room, idly stirring a cup of tea that had already been cold a quarter-hour ago.

"I suppose I have put myself completely beyond the pale," she observed, avoiding the frankly accusing gaze of her hostess. The two ladies were alone in the breakfast room, Amanda being still abed after her night of revelry. By contrast, Morpheus had been unkind to Margaret, leaving her to toss and turn throughout the long watches of the night.

"Indeed, you have." Lady Windhurst reached across the table to still Margaret's restless hand by the simple expedient of covering it with her own. "Delivering the cut direct is not an act that should be done lightly at any time, my dear. When one delivers it to a wealthy and aristocratic gentleman who is also the darling of Society, well, one may hardly expect to emerge unscathed."

Margaret sighed. "I beg your pardon, my lady. It was not my intention to embarrass you, particularly not when you have been so very kind to my sister and me. I was merely taken by surprise. You see, I—the duke and I are already acquainted."

A gleam of ironic humor lit Lady Windhurst's gray eyes, rendering her ladyship a bit less forbidding. "Yes, I rather surmised as much." When Margaret offered no explanation, she prompted, "Perhaps you would feel better for having told me."

Margaret took a deep breath. "I knew him, but not as the duke of Montford. In fact, until quite recently he was a part of my own household. I engaged him myself, to teach Latin to my younger brother. He called himself Mr. Fanshawe." There was more, of course, so much more, but Margaret could not bring herself to speak of it. Indeed, she could hardly bear to think of it without feeling a sudden urge to crawl off into a corner somewhere and howl like a wounded animal.

Her hostess's carefully plucked eyebrows flew upward. "The duke of Montford, teaching Latin under an assumed name? Extraordinary! Have you any idea why he should have sought such a position?"

Margaret shook her head. "None at all."

"What a pity you did not see fit to linger long enough to inquire! I should have loved to hear what he had to say for himself. Oh well, there will be time enough for all that the next time you see him."

"Don't say such a thing, I beg you!" Margaret grimaced at the very thought. "I couldn't—I can't face him again."

"You not only *can,* you *must,*" pronounced Lady Windhurst in a voice which brooked no argument. "You delivered a very public insult to the Toast of the *ton* in full view of a woman whose sobriquet of 'Silence' is not a tribute to her reticence, I assure you! We must do what we can to contain the damage, if you are ever to hold your head up in Town again."

Propping her elbows on the table, Margaret buried her face in her hands. "Believe me, my lady, I have no desire to do so. I only want to go home!"

"And so you shall, eventually, but not until you have ridden out the scandal."

"But how great a scandal can there be? No one even knows me!"

"Perhaps not, but everyone knows the duke, and then there is your sister's approaching wedding to my nephew to consider. You haven't the luxury of indulging your own feelings, my dear."

Mild as this scold was, it affected Margaret with much the same force as a blow to the solar plexus. A scant few weeks earlier, she would have insisted that she had only her sister's best interests at heart; since that time, however, she had discovered herself to be self-deluded. Even the longed-for match between Amanda and the duke (of which she had blithely informed his Grace, she now recalled to her chagrin) had been an indirect acknowledgement that such a personage would be unlikely to harbor matrimonial ambitions toward herself. And then, when the miracle occurred, she had rejected him as ineligible. *Ineligible!*

"I have taken a box at the opera for tomorrow night," Lady Windhurst continued, unmindful of her protégée's inner turmoil. "The duke of Montford, among others, will be invited to join us. You must—you *must!*—be civil to him, no matter the blow to your pride. Remember, all eyes will be upon you."

"Yes, my lady."

A box at the opera, thought Margaret. A darkened box where one must be quiet and fix all one's attention upon the stage. Perhaps it would not be so very bad, after all.

She was wrong. It was torture from the moment he entered the box, greeting her with a tight little bow and a rather uncertain smile.

"Forgive me, Miss Darrington," he murmured, taking the velvet-upholstered chair beside hers, "but if we are to silence the gossips, we must appear to be upon terms."

"The duke of Montford?" She had not known what she would say to him, but this surely was not the most auspicious of beginnings. "That is—I mean—"

"You have every right to be angry with me, but I assure you—"

"Shhhh!" A hush fell over the audience as the lights dimmed and the curtain rose.

"We cannot talk here," James whispered under cover of the opening bars of the overture. "May I call upon you in the morning?"

Margaret struggled with herself. Surely there was nothing he could say, nothing he could do that would lessen her sense of betrayal. And yet, it had seemed for one brief moment as if she had glimpsed plain Mr. Fanshawe beneath the ducal veneer. But that was impossible, she reminded herself. The man she had known as Mr. Fanshawe had never existed. Margaret hardened her heart.

"I cannot see that it would accomplish any useful purpose. Surely prolonging this—this farce would only serve to increase our embarrassment."

Having delivered herself of this unpromising reply, she fixed her attention very pointedly on the stage. Alas, not even the bawdy humor of John Gay's *Beggar's Opera* could prevent her thoughts from straying to the man seated beside her, so near that she might, if she dared, put out her hand and touch him. As if to prevent her from taking any such action, her restless fingers sought refuge in pleating her green satin skirts. And then, as Act I drew to a close, the tenor cast as MacHeath began to sing a familiar lyric. Margaret's fingers clenched, crushing the satin folds. *Were I laid on Greenland's coast, And in my arms embrac'd my lass* . . . It could not be—but of course it was. Part of the reason for the enduring popularity of *The Beggar's Opera* lay in the fact that it incorporated familiar ballads known and sung throughout the length and breadth of England, from formal musical evenings in elegant private homes to boisterous crowds in public taprooms, from stately concert halls to the moonlit terrace of a modest country manor house . . .

And I would love you all the day, If with me you'd fondly stray Over the hills and far away.

Margaret closed her eyes against memories too sweet, too painful to contemplate. She opened them on the second stanza, when the female playing Polly joined in, and surprised on James's face an expression of such anguished longing that her breath caught in her throat. In the next instant it was gone, however, and she was left to wonder if it had ever really been there at all.

Of the ill-assorted group occupying Lady Windhurst's box, only one could truly be said to be enjoying himself. Certainly her ladyship took no pleasure in the comic action onstage, being too concerned with assessing the interaction (if one could call it that) between her young protégée and his Grace. Even Amanda, who usually entered wholeheartedly into anything musical, had bigger fish to fry on this occasion, for having heard, from her sister's lips, the tale of Mr. Fanshawe's masquerade, she now engaged her fiancé in a *sotto voce* lovers' quarrel over his failure to inform her of this interesting development.

Lord Torrington, however, appeared to be in fine fettle, humming tunelessly along with familiar melodies and tapping his foot at apparently random intervals throughout the unfamiliar ones. Between acts, he exerted himself to engage the elder Miss Darrington in light flirtation. To his immense gratification, he was aided in this endeavor by that

187

young lady herself, who found his endless supply of charming trivialities a welcome alternative to the strain of conversing with the man she still could not think of as a duke.

Given so much promising material with which to work, Lord Torrington must perhaps be forgiven for drawing the obvious, albeit entirely erroneous, conclusion.

"James, my lad," he said, dropping by the Montford town house for a brandy before returning to his own rooms in the Albany, "I'm thinking of becoming leg-shackled."

James, decanting the promised beverage into two snifters, looked up with mild interest. "You, married? Surely you jest!"

"Never more serious, I assure you. You will stand up with me in church, will you not?"

"I should consider it an honor," declared James, handing his friend one of the potbellied glasses. "But who, pray, is the unfortunate female upon whom you intend to visit this calamity?"

"The Darrington chit."

"You'll catch cold at that," James cautioned, perching on one corner of an elegant mahogany desk. "She's engaged to Perry. Sorry to disappoint you, old fellow, but I thought you knew."

"Not that one—t'other. Her sister."

James had been idly swirling his brandy around in its snifter, but this pronouncement stayed his hand, leaving both him and the spirituous liquid reeling to find their equilibrium. "You wish to wed *Margaret* Darrington?"

"You find it so hard to believe? Not the diamond her sister is, I'll grant you, but dashed if I don't think her bone structure is superior. She'll age well—better than her sister, mark my words. Besides," he added with simple pride, "I think she fancies me. Don't want to disappoint a lady, you know."

"She—she told you this?"

"Lord, no! A gently bred female wouldn't speak of such things." With a rare flash of sensitivity, Torrington added, "I say, you haven't any objection, have you? Mean to say, I wouldn't want to poach on another fellow's preserves, and all that."

James's smile was bleak, and his voice devoid of all emotion. "No, I—I have no claim on Miss Darrington's affections."

"Just as well, I daresay, for it's as plain as a pikestaff she don't fancy you, not above half." Unaware of having delivered a home thrust, he drained his glass and set it down on the desk. "Now, if you'll excuse me, I'd best toddle on home. I've got a proposal of marriage to make in the morning. Keep a clear head and all that sort of thing, don't you know."

James could not afterwards recall saying goodbye to Lord Torrington, but he must have said all that was proper, for that young man eventually departed, apparently none the wiser, and James was left alone to stare at the brandy still untouched in his glass. *It's plain as a pikestaff she don't fancy you* . . . James could almost envy Torrington his happy obtuseness. What was plain as a pikestaff to James was that Margaret Darrington had once fancied him very much indeed—but not enough, alas, to marry an itinerant tutor without a penny to bless himself with. Oh yes, she might still care for him, but he was not at all certain that, presented with an offer of marriage from a belted earl, his pragmatic love would not put the demands of her purse above the desires of her heart.

James reminded himself that he might have received a

very different answer had he told her the truth while he had the chance. But no, he had been quite determined that she must accept him as plain Mr. Fanshawe. He had claimed a previous disappointment in love as his excuse, but call it by whatever name he would, it all amounted to the same thing—false pride. King Solomon, Sophocles, Heywood—all warned their readers of pride's eventual downfall, and how right they were! He, at least, would find it cold enough comfort when he stood up in church and watched her become Countess of Torrington.

He reached for the bell pull and ordered a new bottle of brandy brought up to the study, then closeted himself therein with his books and his violin. For the next five days, he saw no one, and scarcely touched the food left on a tray every evening outside the study door. Indeed, only the music of the violin drifting through the closed door testified to his presence at all, prompting his housekeeper to say (more than once) that she had served the dukes of Montford for almost thirty years, but if she heard "Over the Hills and Far Away" one more time, she would be forced to give notice.

CHAPTER 15

The sun was setting as the hired post-chaise rolled up the drive to the door of Darrington Place. Aunt Hattie, alone in the stillroom putting up the last of the summer gooseberries, wiped her juice-stained hands on her apron and stepped outside to see who the visitor might be. To her great surprise, the carriage door was thrown open before the wheels stopped moving, and her eldest niece flung herself from the vehicle and into her aunt's arms.

"Margaret! My dear, whatever is the matter?"

For no sooner had Margaret seen the familiar and beloved figure coming forth to greet her than that usually stoic young lady had burst into quite an uncharacteristic display of tears which was now rapidly reducing the front of Aunt Hattie's starched apron to a sodden mess. Thus adjured, Margaret sobbed something incoherent into her aunt's shoulder, of which the only intelligible words were "the duke of Montford."

Aunt Hattie fumbled in her pocket for a shilling for the driver. As the carriage pulled away, she steered Margaret into the house and divested her of bonnet and pelisse as if she were still a very little girl. "Oh, did you meet the duke, then? Tell me, what does he look like?"

This question had the happy effect of enabling Margaret to dry her tears sufficiently to say, "He looks exactly like our own Mr. Fanshawe."

"*Really?*" breathed Aunt Hattie incredulously. "Why, what an *astounding* coincidence!"

In spite of her misery, Margaret was obliged to suppress a smile. "No coincidence, my dear, I assure you. Mr. Fanshawe and the duke of Montford are one and the same. He deceived me. He deceived us all."

"Oh. Oh, dear. I suppose I should have known."

"Nonsense! Why should you?"

Aunt Hattie twisted her hands in her apron. "Because, you see, I had a letter from Mr. Fanshawe—the real Mr. Fanshawe, that is. It seems he was very ill and could not come to us, and somehow our Mr. Fanshawe—the duke, I should say, although I must say that sounds very odd—took his place."

"Are you telling me that you *knew* he was not really Mr. Fanshawe?"

"Yes, but the poor boy begged me so pitifully not to tell that I put the letter in the fire."

"Aunt Hattie, how could you? Why, we might have been murdered in our beds!"

"Nonsense! Anyone could see dear Mr. Fanshawe would never hurt a fly. That is, the duke would not; as for the real Mr. Fanshawe, I'm sure I don't know, for I never had the opportunity to meet him, but you checked out his references very thoroughly, and if you deemed him a suitable man to have charge of our Philip, then I'm sure—"

"Aunt Hattie, why didn't you tell me he was the duke?"

"Oh, but I didn't know! Very slow-witted of me, I'm sure, for he has the Weatherly nose. I daresay I was led astray on account of his being so very fair, when the Weatherlys are always dark. I wonder if he can be a throw-back to poor Lord Robert's dairymaid? I believe she was reckoned to be very beautiful."

"But Auntie, you should have told me that Mr. Fanshawe was—was not who we believed him to be!"

"I suppose I should have, but we had all grown quite fond of him by that time, and Philip was doing so well with his studies, so what harm could there be in keeping him?"

"You cannot 'keep' a human being as you would a stray cat!" protested Margaret, torn between exasperation and amusement. "And as it turns out, there was indeed harm—indelible, irreparable harm."

"If that is true, my dear, I am sorry for it," said Aunt Hattie, looking chastened. "But what—?"

Margaret, awash with shame at the memory, raised a hand to her eyes as if to block out the painful image. "I very obligingly informed Mr. Fanshawe of my hopes that Amanda might make our fortunes by marrying the duke."

"Embarrassing for you, I am sure, but since Amanda and dear Peregrine are so very happy together, I hardly see why—"

"There is more," confessed Margaret. "Mr. Fanshawe asked me to marry him."

"Margaret!" breathed Aunt Hattie, wreathed in smiles. "Oh, my love—"

Margaret hung her head. "I refused him."

"*Refused?*" echoed her aunt, stricken. "But *why?* You may well tell me I should mind my own business, but it always seemed to me that you had a marked partiality for him."

"Surely you must see that 'partiality,' or the lack of it, has nothing to say to the matter! How could I in good conscience have accepted a proposal from a man with an income of no more than thirty-five pounds per annum—an income paid, I might add, out of my own father's estate?"

Shaking her head sadly, Aunt Hattie made a little clicking sound with her tongue, putting her niece forcibly in mind of the plump hens that scratched about the stable yard. "It all sounds very logical, my dear, but I cannot think it wise. In my experience, love comes in short enough supply that one can ill afford to throw it away. But now that he is a duke, surely you can have no objections to him?"

"I fear it is too late for that. I made it quite plain that I would not listen to his proposal, and if that were not enough, my conduct toward him in London was such as surely must have given him a disgust of me."

"Disgust? My dear Margaret, what did you do?"

"I—I seem to have given him the cut direct."

Aunt Hattie fell back in her chair with a moan and fumbled for her smelling salts.

"So you see," Margaret concluded, "it is unlikely that he will offer for me again."

Unlikelihood notwithstanding, Margaret still found herself, in the long and lonely days that followed, gazing out the window at the Palladian house on the hill and searching for some indication that the new duke had taken up residence there. She knew this to be an exercise in futility, for why should he pursue her into the country when he had all London at his ducal feet? And yet, in spite of this unassailable logic, her frequent walks inevitably led to the shell of the old priory, from which vantage point the best view of the more modern structure might be obtained. *It might have been yours,* her heart silently accused. She might have lived the rest of her life within those spacious, elegantly appointed rooms, entertaining the local ladies to tea by day, and presiding over lavish dinner parties at night. More importantly, *he* might have been hers, filling her days with violin music, while as for the nights. . . .

Her imagination shied away from thoughts wholly inappropriate to gently bred unmarried ladies. She wrested her mind firmly back to the present, and was surprised to find long shadows striping the ground with purple and gold. The darkness fell earlier now, as the mild days of autumn began their yearly surrender to the bleak winter. If she stayed out too late, Aunt Hattie would worry. She carefully picked her way back through the crumbled stones, suddenly eager to be free of the ancient ruins. This was indeed a haunted place, but she had no fear of long-departed monks or abbots. No, it was another sort of specter, very much alive, who haunted her thoughts and disturbed her dreams.

So constant was his presence in her thoughts that, when she came within sight of Darrington House and saw standing in the drive a sleek black carriage bearing a crest on its panel, she felt as if all the misery of the last week had been but a prelude to this moment. With pounding heart, she resisted the urge to run the rest of the way to the house, forcing herself instead to walk sedately up the drive.

No sooner had she stepped onto the porch than the front door was flung open by an agitated Tilly. "Oh, Miss Margaret, thank heaven you've come! There's a fine gentleman come all the way from London to see you!"

"Thank you, Tilly," Margaret replied, feigning a composure she was far from feeling. "You may tell him I shall be with him directly."

She waited until the maid had taken herself off to deliver the message, then turned to the mirror and began raking frantic fingers through her wind-ravaged tresses. The one time she went outside without a bonnet, and now this! She pinched quite unnecessary color into cheeks already rosy from exertion and suppressed emotion, then clasping her hands tightly together, joined her guest in the drawing room.

She blinked at the sight of the gentleman who rose at her

entrance. This was no golden-haired duke, but a vaguely familiar young man whose curled and pomaded locks and excruciatingly fashionable attire suggested an inclination toward dandyism.

"Your servant, Miss Darrington," said this individual, bowing from the waist.

The sound of his voice had the happy effect of allowing her to fix him in her memory. This was the earl of Torrington, with whom she had made desperate conversation in an attempt to avoid the duke of Montford's all too disturbing presence. Certainly gratitude demanded that his lordship be given a warmer greeting than he had thus far received.

"My lord, how—how very good to see you," she said, hastening to offer her hand. "But I had thought you fixed in Town. Tell me, what brings you to Montford?"

In fact, Torrington was beginning to wonder that very thing himself. When in London, it had been very well to contemplate marriage with an elegantly gowned and coiffed Unknown; now, however, he found himself confronted with a country lass whose faded gown and sturdy shoes (to say nothing of her ruddy cheeks and windblown hair) suggested that she had been occupied outdoors without so much as a bonnet. His fastidious soul recoiled from the very suggestion. He could not entirely approve of the outdoors even on the mildest of days; the sun wreaked such havoc with one's complexion. A charitable fellow by nature, he allowed that Miss Darrington's transgressions might be excused by ignorance; he even admitted that there was a certain appeal in the prospect of molding a country mouse into a fashionable countess. Alas, the brief time he had spent in Miss Darrington's company had given him the impression that, far from being moldable, she was more likely to prove a frighteningly competent young woman who knew her own mind. For the first time since his conversation with James, he began to wonder if he was being a bit hasty.

But one could hardly admit as much to a young lady for whose sake he had made the journey from London for the express purpose of proposing marriage. So he took her proffered hand—she was not wearing gloves, he noted with some consternation—and raised it to his lips, saying, "Can you doubt it? I came to see you."

Margaret smiled. "Very prettily said, my lord. Do sit down! Shall I ring for tea?"

"No, no," he said hastily, quaking inwardly at the prospect of going down on one knee while simultaneously juggling a cup and saucer of boiling hot liquid. "I ate at the posting-house—the Pig and Whistle."

"Then you are spending the night in Montford," deduced Margaret, who had supposed her guest to be merely paying a courtesy call on his way to some other place. "Do you anticipate a long stay?"

Torrington, settling himself on one end of the sofa, merely shrugged. "Maybe, maybe not. Just wanted to get out of London for a spell. Veritable desert without you, and all that, don't you know."

Margaret raised a skeptical eyebrow. "Now, *that* I beg leave to doubt, given your wide acquaintance amongst the *ton*." She knew she should not, but she could no more stop herself asking than she could stop her heart beating. "Tell me, how goes our mutual friend, the duke of Montford?"

"Oh, swimmingly," Lord Torrington assured her blithely. "Expect his engagement to be announced any day now—might be betrothed by this time, for all I know."

Margaret's hand went instinctively to her bosom, as if to clutch at the knife that had just been plunged into her heart. "Miss—Miss Prescott is very beautiful," she said, noting with detached surprise how very calm her voice sounded, when inwardly she wanted to sob and wail.

Torrington might not have noticed if she had done so, for by this time the earl had seen his opening and was determined to follow through with his proposal before he lost his nerve entirely.

"Got me thinking about my own bachelor state," he continued. "High time I settled down, set up my nursery—ensured the succession and all that, don't you know."

Margaret, concentrating on taking deep, steadying breaths, made no reply.

"Well?" prompted the earl, slipping off the sofa and onto one knee. "What do you say? Will you do me the honor of becoming my wife?"

Margaret, lost in a waking nightmare in which she was obliged to dine at Montford Priory, during which meal James and his blushing bride made sheep's eyes at one another down the length of the dinner table, was wrested back to the present so abruptly that she was left gasping for breath, much like a swimmer who has remained too long under water. "I—I beg your pardon?"

"Asking you to marry me—be my countess, and all that."

"I—I hardly know what to say," stammered Margaret, dazed by this unexpected turn of events. She had dreamed of a brilliant marriage for her sister; she never once considered that she might make one herself.

"Just say 'yes,' " suggested the earl.

It was as simple as that. As the Countess of Torrington, she would have wealth and position for herself and financial security for her family. It was all she had ever wanted. Granted, his veneer of fashionable affectation made it difficult to know precisely what sort of man the earl was, but she knew him to be good-natured, and although he was far from astute, she did not think him entirely lacking in intelligence. She was sure he would make a kind and generous husband. Any woman would be mad to refuse such an advantageous match. And yet, somehow, it was no longer enough.

"I fear that is the one thing I can never say, my lord."

"Too soon—rushed my fences," acknowledged Torrington, nodding in sympathy. "Take some time—think about it."

"You are most generous, but it would be wrong of me to encourage you to hope. I am deeply aware of the honor you do me, my lord, but I cannot marry you."

"I see," said the earl, rising from his kneeling position and carefully brushing the creases from the knees of his breeches. "Someone else, perhaps?"

"Yes, that is it," agreed Margaret, grateful for his ready understanding. "You deserve better than a wife whose heart belongs to another."

"Anyone I know? What I mean to say is, if there's anything I can do—"

"Thank you, but no. It all happened before I came to London, you see." She smiled sadly. "His name was Mr. Fanshawe."

CHAPTER 16

Upon his return to London, Lord Torrington presented himself at the front door of the duke of Montford's town house only to be informed by the butler that his Grace was not seeing visitors.

"He'll see me," the earl predicted with the ease of long acquaintance.

Brushing past the butler unmindful of that individual's protests, he followed the sound of violin music up the stairs and down the corridor to the study. Finding the door locked, he rapped sharply upon it with the brass head of his ebony walking stick. When no one opened the door, he pounded upon it with his fists.

"Yes, yes, I'm coming," came a muffled voice from within.

A moment later, the knob rattled and the door swung open. It was indeed James, but no one who had seen the elegant young duke at Almack's would have recognized him in the haggard individual who held the doorknob in one hand and a battered violin in the other. His creased and disheveled clothing bore all the appearance of having been slept in, and his unknotted cravat hung loosely about his neck. His hair was uncombed, and his chin sported several days' growth of blond beard.

"Torry!" he exclaimed, his bloodshot eyes blazing to life. "Gad, man, what's taken you so long?"

"Had to chase my chosen bride into the wilds of Surrey. Dash it, old thing, how long since you've shaved?"

"Never mind that! Did she—am I to wish you happy?"

Torrington shook his head. " 'Fraid not. Turned me down flat."

"She *turned you down?*" echoed James, afraid to hope.

"Flat," repeated the earl. "Said she couldn't marry where she didn't love."

"*Miss Darrington* said that? Not—you are quite sure—not Miss *Amanda* Darrington?"

"No, no, Miss Margaret Darrington, 'pon rep. Said she loved another, and would marry no one else. You wouldn't know him—fellow by the name of Fanshawe."

"Fanshawe? Did you say *Fanshawe?*" Casting his violin aside, James brushed past the earl and mounted the steps to the second floor two at a time. "Good God, I'm ravenous! Why hasn't my staff given me anything to eat? Doggett? *Doggett!* Ah, there you are! My razor, if you please, and pack my bags for an extended journey. Sorry to abandon you, Torry, but I must away to Montford to claim my inheritance and my bride—although not necessarily in that order."

"But I thought you were to marry the Prescott chit," protested Torrington, standing at the foot of the stairs. "And what about this Fanshawe fellow?"

James, having already reached the landing and made the turn, leaned over the railing. "*I* am Mr. Fanshawe!"

"Dash it all, my lad," expostulated the bewildered earl, "I thought your family name was Weatherly!"

"Are you quite sure you will not come with me, Margaret?" asked Aunt Hattie as she tied the ribbons of her bonnet. "I am sure such an intelligent creature as you are would be a valuable addition to the Ladies' Missionary Aid Society."

Margaret, curled up on the window seat with a book, looked up from the printed page and shook her head. "Thank you, Aunt Hattie, but I should prefer to remain quietly at home." Seeing her aunt was still not convinced, she managed a wan smile. "I assure you, I will not expire of a broken heart in your absence."

"No, for hearts are not so cooperative, are they?" the older woman observed ruefully. "Still, I wonder if it is quite good for you to spend so very much time alone."

"Tell me, Aunt Hattie, was I wrong to decline Lord Torrington's offer?" Margaret's eyes were clouded with anguished indecision. "I might have come to love him in time."

"Indeed, you might have, but I think it much more likely that you would have come to resent him for being himself, instead of the man you wanted him to be. No, dearest, I think you were right to refuse him. There may be days when you wish you had married him, it is true. And yet it seems better to me that one regret the things one did *not* do than to regret things one has done and cannot *un*do, if you see what I mean."

Margaret, following this convoluted sentence with some difficulty, rose from the window seat to embrace her aunt. "I see exactly what you mean, and I think you must be right. Oh, Aunt Hattie, I wish I were as wise as you."

"Wise?" echoed her aunt incredulously. "Me? Why, your papa was used to say I was the greatest pea-goose of his acquaintance! Will you not come with me? I can promise you a very busy morning with little time for blue megrims, for today we are making candles to send to the natives in darkest Africa."

"Perhaps another time. Only tell me, Aunt Hattie. I am sure you are rendering a valuable service, but—why candles?"

"You cannot have been paying attention, my love," chided Aunt Hattie. "*Darkest* Africa, you know! Now, what have I said to make you laugh? Never mind, I don't want to know. I am only pleased to see you happy again."

On this note Aunt Hattie took her leave, bearing her basket of candle-making supplies on her arm. Left to her own devices, Margaret returned to her reading, but not even Mrs. Radcliffe's ghostly monks, haunted abbeys, and fainting heroines were sufficient to prevent her mind from wandering back to a certain golden-haired Latin scholar, and the joy that might have been hers. Half an hour had passed in this manner (during which time she had read the same paragraph four times without yet comprehending it) when the sound of the door knocker shattered the silence.

Margaret was surprised in more ways than one, for in addition to being startled out of her reverie, she could not think who might be calling at such a time, when most of her aunt's friends were making candles with the Ladies' Missionary Aid Society. She waited for Tilly to announce the caller, but the maid never came. Instead, a second knock sounded, this one louder and longer than the first.

"Tilly?" Margaret called. "Tilly, someone is at the door."

When no footsteps hurried to answer the summons, Margaret remembered this was Tilly's marketing day. If the door were to be opened, Margaret would have to do it herself. Casting her neglected book aside, she shook out her skirts and reached the door just as a third knock sounded. She seized the knob, turned it, and pulled.

There on the porch stood a tall, almost gangly young man clad in an outmoded coat whose sleeves did not quite cover his wrists. Although his garments were depressingly sober-hued, his golden hair shone in the autumn sunlight, and behind his wire-rimmed spectacles, his eyes were a brilliant blue.

"Mr. Fan—that is, your Grace," stammered Margaret, sinking into a deep curtsy.

"Miss Darrington," he said, answering her curtsy with a bow, "I understand you have a position available for which I wish to be considered."

Whatever she had expected him to say, it was not that. "I—we—Philip is quite happy at school, and doing very well there," she said, nonplussed. "We have no need of a tutor."

"The position I am applying for," he continued, "is that of your husband."

Margaret, still holding the door, now clutched at it for support, lest her knees give way beneath her. "Really, Mr.— your Grace, one can hardly engage a husband as one might a butler, or a—a—"

"A tutor?" James suggested, smiling his dimpled smile. "You have no idea how relieved I am to hear you say so. You have more than once given me to understand that was *exactly* how one should go about the business."

The dimples almost undid her. "Your Grace, I am painfully aware of having said any number of—of foolish things to you," she said, choking back tears of humiliation and heartbreak. "I beg you will cease making a May-game of me by throwing them in my face."

She at least had the satisfaction of seeing the smile wiped from his face. "Is that why you think I've come all the way from London? Good God, what a pretty fellow you must think me!"

"How should I know what to think of you? I don't even know you!"

But even as she said the words, she knew they were not

true. She knew him, had known him almost from the moment she had first seen him bloody and beaten in the road, with the instinctive knowledge of the heart recognizing its soul mate. It would make no difference whether he called himself Mr. Fanshawe, or the duke of Montford, or the Czar of all the Russias.

Still, there were things that must be said, questions that must be asked. Days, weeks of agony were summed up in half a dozen words. "Why did you never tell me?"

He expelled a deep breath. "I fear it makes for a rather long story. The short version is, I didn't know it myself—at least, not at first. I had just arrived in Montford to claim my inheritance when I was set upon by footpads—but you know that part. What you don't know was that their tender ministrations were sufficient to deprive me of my memory. When you came along, apparently expecting me, I assumed I must be your Mr. Fanshawe. I labored under that delusion for several weeks, until our visit to Montford Priory. A certain silhouette there bore such a marked resemblance to Miss Amanda's handiwork that it brought everything rushing back."

"But you said nothing, even then!"

"No, for to have done so would have been extremely awkward for all of us. Besides, your family had taken me in and nursed my wounds—and loved me a little, I think. In some ways, you became the family I never had. I was in no hurry to give all that up for a life of lonely luxury."

"We would have come to visit you—"

"I can see us now, very properly sipping tea under Aunt Hattie's chaperonage. I thank you, but no!" He hesitated a moment before adding, "There was another reason, too, in which my rôle is not nearly so heroic. Before I came to Montford, I was curate of a rural parish. There I fell in love—or thought I did—with one of the daughters of the local gentry."

"Miss Prescott?" breathed Margaret.

"The very same. I asked her to marry me, and was promptly turned down. She was very beautiful, as you know, and her sights were set much higher than a shabby-genteel curate with no prospects. So she went to London, and I—" His mouth twisted in a wry smile. "I inherited a dukedom."

"So you might have married her after all."

"True. But I had learned a hard lesson, which left me determined not to be married for the sake of my title. And so it was as plain Mr. Fanshawe, rather than the duke of Montford, that I asked you to marry me. When I met with much the same response, I told myself I had been wise to withhold the information, and went off to London to lick my wounds and make my mark in Society." He possessed himself of her hands. "So there you have it. I have been both a pauper and a peer, but I find I would rather be a tutor with you than a duke without you. I am not mistaken, am I, in thinking that you—care for me—to some extent?"

"No." Her confession was scarcely more than a whisper. "No, you are not mistaken. It was not until the night Amanda's betrothal was announced that I realized why I was so set against your marrying her. For one dreadful moment, you see, I—I thought it was you."

He released her hands, but only so that he might take her into his arms. "My dearest love!"

"But I can never marry you now," Margaret said some time later, emerging flushed and breathless from his kiss. "Not after I refused to have you as plain Mr. Fanshawe. What sort of person would that make me?"

"Human," he suggested. "Imperfectly, adorably human."

"Everyone would say I only married you in order to become the duchess of Montford," she insisted. "And they would call you a fool for allowing yourself to be entrapped by a country nobody."

He merely shrugged. "So they may. But we'll be halfway up the Acropolis by that time. We won't hear a thing."

As a diversionary tactic, it worked brilliantly. "Oh, do you remember that?" she exclaimed, gazing up at him with a singularly foolish smile playing about her mouth.

"I remember everything you ever said to me, up to and including the bit about Aunt Hattie and the naked Romans." His tone was playful, but there was a light in his blue eyes that made her feel suddenly weak in the knees. "I want to kiss you on the steps of the Parthenon, Margaret. I want to explore the Coliseum hand in hand with you, and swim naked with you in a Roman bath."

"Oh!" she exclaimed, blushing rosily.

"And then," he went on, unmindful of her maidenly modesty, "I want to settle down in the Priory and set about ensuring the succession." He grinned sheepishly. "It is truly amazing how quickly one adapts to a dynastic mode of thinking. Tell me, shall we engage an artist from the Royal Academy to restore the Hogarth? I think I should like our children to know their great-grandfather."

"*I* should settle for knowing their father," she retorted. "Do you realize that I don't even know your name? I can no longer call you Mr. Fanshawe, and I refuse to go through life addressing my husband as 'your Grace.' "

"No, too formal by half, particularly in moments of, er, connubial bliss," he agreed. "When we are in private, a simple 'duke' will suffice."

"Oh, you *are* an idiot," she said with a blissful sigh.

"Not at all. Mr. Fanshawe may have been an idiot, but now I am a duke, and therefore merely eccentric. And incidentally, my name is James."

"Are you certain? I should hate for you to suddenly remember another identity, along with perhaps a wife and six children somewhere, all awaiting your return."

"No, no other wife and children. I am quite certain I am James Weatherly—just as I am certain that I love you, Margaret Darrington."

He would have taken her into his arms to demonstrate the truth of this statement, but she splayed her hands against his chest, holding him off.

"But James, darling, are you quite sure you wish to marry me? You may find yourself living under the cat's paw, for I fear I shall always be an odiously *managing* sort of female!"

"Oh, I've no doubt of it! Fortunately, it so happens that my dearest wish is to be managed by you for the rest of my life. Now kiss me, my love, or I shall suspect that your only interest in me lies in my coronet."

Margaret, determined to refute so unjust a charge, obeyed with enthusiasm.

About the Author

Sheri Cobb South has loved the Regency genre ever since she discovered Georgette Heyer at the age of sixteen. Her Regency novels include the award-winning *Miss Darby's Duenna* and *French Leave*, as well as the Regency-set mystery *In Milady's Chamber*. In addition to reading and writing, Sheri enjoys needlework, singing, playing the clarinet, and watching old movies. She is a graduate *summa cum laude* of the University of South Alabama, where she earned a BA in English. Sheri lives in Mobile, Alabama, with her family, and loves to hear from readers. She may be contacted at Cobbsouth@aol.com.